Meticulous, Sad and Lonely

Stories by Ian Roy

BuschekBooks
Ottawa

Copyright©2015 Ian Roy
All rights reserved

Library and Archives Canada Cataloguing in Publication

Roy, Ian, 1972-, author
 Meticulous, sad and lonely : stories / Ian Roy.

ISBN 978-1-894543-86-6 (paperback)

 I. Title.

PS8585.O89835M48 2015 C813'.6 C2015-906745-6

Illustrations & cover design by Jon Claytor
Author photograph by Max Caspi-Roy

Printed in Winnipeg, Manitoba, Canada by Hignell Book Printing.

BuschekBooks
P.O. Box 74053
5 Beechwood Avenue
Ottawa, Ontario, Canada K1M 2H9
www.buschekbooks.com

For Max and Ari

Contents

The Brothers 7
Clouds 9
Gravity 13
Suit 15
Meticulous, Sad and Lonely 19
The Lion and The Writer 25
When Mother Loved The Bear 27
The Funeral 35
Tony MacFuckingDougall 37
5 Cents 41
Here's The Kicker 47
Luke and Pearl and Jonas and Fifty 49
Her Name is January 57
This is What Happened When I Died 59
There's a Little Black Spot 63
Births, Deaths and Marriages 69
Divorce 73
My Dead Father 83
Flood 85
The Sisters 91
The Three Napoleons 93
Beats Sitting In a Cage All Day 103

Acknowledgements 106

THE BROTHERS

So there were two brothers. A quiet one and one that was, frankly, not so quiet. As a matter of fact, he never stopped talking. This one even talked in his sleep.

The talking brother would go on and on about absolutely nothing. He just liked to hear himself speak. And the other brother, the quiet one, well, he had been putting up with this for a long time. And he had had enough.

For the past seven years, the quiet brother had been trying to read the same book. But he just couldn't make any progress with this book because of all the talking. So one day while his voluble brother was going on again with the talking, and the inane stories and all of that, the quiet brother led him up onto the roof of their house. It was not hard to do. He just climbed up there and his brother followed, still talking. That's how it always went: the quiet brother trying to escape, and the chatty brother following him around the house, talking and talking.

There was a nice breeze on the roof. The moon was rising over the neighbour's house. The first few stars were visible in the night sky. It was that kind of night. But the quiet brother couldn't enjoy any of this because of the incessant talking. He walked his brother to the edge of the roof and pointed at the horizon. And then—this is so terrible but he really didn't know what else to do—without a single word, he pushed his brother. Really hard. The thing is, the talking brother didn't fall to the ground. No, he went soaring through the air like a bird, like a hawk gliding on a wind current, like a hang-glider with no hang-glider. And all the while, he kept on talking. It's possible that he didn't even realize that he was flying through the air. The last thing the quiet brother heard him say was, Don't get your hopes up. He'd been talking about sharing his lottery winnings—if ever he should win.

Before long, that talkative brother cleared the last house on the street and was out of sight.

The other brother, the quiet one, went back inside the house and sat down on his favourite chair. He picked up his book and blew the dust off the cover. He watched the dust swirl and settle in the lamp light. He now had time for this kind of quiet observation. He smiled; he was pretty pleased with himself. He turned the book over and then back again, taking it all in, weighing its heft in his hands. It was a thick book, written by a Russian author over a hundred years earlier. And it was about brothers. The quiet brother removed the bookmark from where it had remained all that time and he began reading.

CLOUDS

Adele decided that the worst thing about the party was not her sister's smug boyfriend who smelled like an unholy combination of garlic and musk scented cologne, nor was it the food, which was uninspired and really more church-basement-pot-luck than dinner party, right down to the devilled eggs and cheese balls; and it wasn't the fact that there had not been a single cloud in the sky for over nine months, and people were starting to worry because that kind of thing didn't happen in Montreal—ever; and it also wasn't the fact that Adele had recently become single again and, well, jobless, too, and that certainly did not inspire party-time in Adele. No, it was none of those things in particular, though they didn't help her state of mind in the least. Especially this thing about the clouds; she was becoming increasingly anxious about that situation. Couldn't the earth burn up, killing everyone and everything? She made a note to herself to look that up when she got home. Worse than all of this, Adele concluded, was that Jackie was hosting it on the anniversary of their granny's death, and Jackie had made no effort whatsoever to acknowledge the day for what it was; and Adele, being stubborn and also sad, waited impatiently for her sister to say something about it, though she knew Jackie probably didn't even remember.

    Adele awoke that morning wanting to substitute her usual cup of coffee for a glass of red wine. With her head on the pillow, and her eyes still closed, she could easily picture the bottle of Shiraz on the kitchen counter. Saturday morning, and it was still uncorked. A miracle. After all, it had been a long, difficult week. Oh, who was she kidding? She bought four bottles on Wednesday. That orphaned bottle of Shiraz was the last one standing. And only because she was supposed to take it to Jackie's dinner party, otherwise…. She turned away from the harsh light coming in the window, and opened her eyes a little. She ran her tongue along her dry lips, almost tasting the wine. The word decorum popped into her head. Decorum, in turn, made her think of the word disdain. And then disappointment. She sighed. All of these words already, and it wasn't even a weekday.

In the kitchen, she settled for a cup of coffee. And, fifteen minutes later, a second cup. She sat at the table with a list in front of her. Make spinach dip for the party. Pick up a loaf of rye bread. For the party. Check Workopolis. Check Craigslist for a new apartment. She thought again about the bottle of wine. Her glass from the night before was still on the table. A dead drunk fruit fly floated at the bottom of the glass. She pushed it across the table. She could always pick up another bottle of wine for the party when she was out. She got a clean glass out of the cupboard. And then spent fifteen minutes fishing the corkscrew out of that no-man's-land between the stove and counter where it had fallen the night before.

Decorum.

There was that word again. She wrote it down at the bottom of her list, right under wash underwear in bathroom sink.

While waiting at the bus stop to go to Jackie's, a woman approached Adele with both of her hands down the front of her pants.

—Do I know you? The woman asked Adele.

—I don't think so, said Adele. She was actually quite certain.

—Are you my sister?

—No, said Adele, I'm not… Sorry.

—Sometimes she plays tricks on me, the woman continued. And it could be that you are her playing a trick on me right now.

—No, Adele said again, I am not your sister.

The woman was quiet. But she did not move, or turn away. Instead, she stared into Adele's eyes for too long.

—We have the same eyes, you and me. Just exactly the same, said the woman.

She took her hands out of her pants, and pointed from her own eyes to Adele's. Adele looked into the woman's eyes. They were almost aquamarine in colour. Adele's eyes were brown. Well, hazel. But mostly brown. And definitely not aquamarine.

—That's uncanny, said Adele looking at the woman's tired blue eyes. She could see now, looking closer, that they were kind of milky and unfocused. Adele realized that maybe the woman was not talking about the colour at all.

—Where are the clouds? The woman asked. Where did they all go? Adele just shook her head.

The woman put her hands back in her pants and walked off, muttering to herself. It was only then that Adele noticed she was barefoot.

She reminded Adele of her granny near the end of her life. She was always saying things like that; and taking her clothes off in public. Adele began to cry. She put her bag down on the dirty sidewalk and rummaged in it until she found her sunglasses. She put them on just as the bus arrived.

The ride was not nearly long enough. And when Adele got to the party, she had to endure her sister making a big production of Adele having arrived alone. Jackie looked up and down the street dramatically, hand held to her forehead as if she were standing on a ship's bow, searching for Adele's date—knowing, of course, that Adele had recently broken up with her boyfriend. Who, exactly, Jackie was expecting to see there on the street, Adele did not know. All she wanted was for Jackie to remember their granny, to say she remembered. It hadn't really been that long at all; not long enough to be having a party that wasn't in memory of her. But she wouldn't; Jackie just wouldn't. So Adele went inside and endured being introduced to everyone by a spiteful and oblivious Jackie.

—This is Bob and Tracy. They've been married for twelve years. A dozen! And this is their son Colon.

Colon? That couldn't be right, thought Adele. She must have misheard. She smiled sadly at the kid. He was sure to get beat up with a name like that.

Jackie continued.

—This is Earl and his fiancée, Jessica. Mazel tov, you two! And of course you know Denny and his partner Alex. They're adopting a girl from China next month. We're so excited for them!

Are we? Adele wanted to ask.

—You can sit here, beside Josh, my captain, my prince.

Adele gagged audibly.

Josh rolled his eyes and shimmied his chair a few inches away from Adele's.

By the time dessert was served, Adele was a little bit drunk, sure, and seething—not with anger, but with exhaustion. Was that even possible? She thought so, yes. And everyone sat around the table talking and talking. And Jackie sat there presiding over all of them like some grand dame. And probably quietly—or not so quietly—judging Adele. And for what? Because

11

she was the only single person at the party? Because she was let go from another job?

—People, Adele said out loud without at first realizing that she was talking out loud, people lose their jobs all the frigging time.

Everyone around the table stopped talking and looked from Adele to Jackie, and then back to Adele.

She very slowly and very deliberately unbuttoned all the buttons on her blouse. She pulled it off, and let it fall to the floor.

—And most of those people are decent, honest people, Adele said, stepping up onto her chair. They just got a bad break somewhere along the way.

She knew she wasn't really drunk enough to be doing what she was doing. But she stood there anyway. Across from her, Bob and Tracy's ten or eleven year-old son—What was his name? Callum? Colin? It started with a C—whatever his name was, he was staring at Adele's left breast. She thought it strange that he'd focus on just the left one. She looked down. And there, in the cup covering her left breast, was a small tear in the fabric. On the side a little, not over her nipple and not over the star shaped mole above and to the right of her nipple.

—I guess, she said, I'm having a wardrobe malfunction.

It began to feel like a lot of time had passed. And she really didn't have anything else to say. She looked around the table. The guests just stared at her, unspeaking. Jackie's eyes were narrow slits, and her lips were pursed so tight that her mouth, Adele observed, looked like a cat's arse.

—Your mouth, said Adele, reminds me of a cat's arse.

Jackie did not smile, did not even blink.

—Okay, then. Adele stepped down from her chair. All righty, I'm going to go now. Young man, she addressed the boy whose name started with a C, not a word about this to your classmates.

The boy looked scared. His mother put her arm around his shoulders.

Adele picked up her blouse. And walked out of the room. And then out of the house. And down the front steps and out onto the sidewalk where she finally stopped to put on her blouse.

A young couple stood at the bus stop across the street, watching her. Adele smiled at the two of them and looked up at the starry sky. There was not a cloud in sight. How long could this go on?

—I'm a cloud, she said to the young couple at the bus stop. I am a cloud on a cloudless night. And that right there is the saddest thing in the world. Tonight, anyway. Tomorrow night, something else will take its place. But for tonight... that's the saddest thing in the world.

Adele did up the last button on her blouse and walked all the way home.

GRAVITY

They flipped the gravity, and everything fell to the ceiling. It was pretty funny, unless you were outside. I saw a couple holding hands fall into the sky. They were fucked. Usually there was a warning. When the sirens go off, you have exactly five minutes to get yourself strapped into one of the anti-gravity-harness-units that are all over the compound. Inside, most things are stuck to surfaces. And what isn't stuck or held in place with Velcro or glue or whatever they use, is made of or surrounded by elastic-membrane. So things bounce off the ceiling.

    They do it to recalibrate the system. I'm not sure what that even means but there you go. It's something they've been developing for a while. They're so proud of it but I really have no idea of its purpose. If you ask me, it's stupid.

    The transition from gravity to no-gravity usually happens slowly, so that you sort of float to the ceiling. That way you don't get hurt. It never lasts very long. Although one time I remember it was about an hour. It got kind of boring. There is only so much to do on the ceiling of your unit. Most days it's a few minutes out of your day, tops. And then the sirens to warn you that it's switching back. No harm, no foul.

    This time, though, there was no warning. I'm pretty sure they're fucking with us.

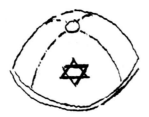

SUIT

He was standing outside of his suit store on the corner of Orchard and Grand. A short round man with greying, curly hair and a kippah that just barely hid a bald spot. His shirt sleeves were rolled up, revealing smooth, hairless arms. He had short, thick fingers that would have made my old piano teacher cry. They were the hands of a boxer but there was no way this man was or ever had been a boxer. If I had to guess, I'd say he'd been selling suits his entire life. He held out his hand and introduced himself as Moshe.

He gestured to my beard and said, A trim wouldn't hurt.

—What's the point, I asked?

—Young ladies like a trimmed beard.

—Young ladies, I said, also like running off with other men.

—Ah, he said, nodding his head. I see, I see. He hadn't yet let go of my hand.

He was quiet for a moment, and with my hand held limp in his, he looked into my eyes. It took me all of four seconds—I counted—before I looked away.

Moshe's shoes were brown and freshly polished. His pants, expertly hemmed.

His grip wasn't tight but it wasn't loose, either. I gave his hand a shake and tried releasing my fingers from his grasp but, still holding my hand in his, Moshe put his left hand on my shoulder and led me into his store.

The store, empty of customers, was full of suits, suits and little else. Most were grey. Or blue or black or brown. One or two were beige. There were some shirts, too, more colourful than the suits. And ties, also colourful. A glass cabinet by the antique cash register held some dusty cufflinks. The carpet looked as though it had neither been replaced nor cleaned in more years than I'd been alive. It was littered with straight pins.

Moshe, rolling down his shirt sleeves, followed my gaze.

—I can't run the vacuum because the pins puncture the bag.

Shirt sleeves rolled down and a jacket now on and buttoned, Moshe guided me across the room to a rack of grey and blue and black and brown suits. I still owned the suit I'd worn to my bar mitzvah fourteen years earlier. It still fit. Or I could still get it on, at any rate. I'd worn it to a wedding the previous summer, upstate, surrounded by one thousand disappointed relatives. I looked precisely like a grown man wearing a boy's suit. My own mother told me as much. A wife you will never find wearing a suit like that, she said. I reminded her that she was the one who bought me the suit in the first place. I bought that suit for a boy, she said, not a man. A boy.

Looking me up and down, Moshe asked, Who is the smartest man on earth?

—Not me, I said.

—That is absolutely the answer I was looking for, he said. It took me years—years!—to arrive at that answer. And you, what, a man of twenty-five?

—Twenty-seven.

—A man of twenty-seven, and here you are, a mind open to the wonders of the universe and the limitations of mankind. My own grown children, I ask them every day: Who is the smartest man on earth? And they still answer this man or that man—a president, a scientist. The girls, they say, Our mother, that's who. And they have a point.

He was walking his fingers along some jackets on a rack and glancing at me now and then.

—But knowing that one knows very little of what there is to know is a step towards knowing more of what there is to know, a step towards happiness.

—Aren't the two mutually exclusive?

—Ah. His fingers stopped walking across the shoulders of the hanging jackets. That kind of thinking is a step backward!

His fingers continued as though searching for a file folder.

—Do you know what would be perfect for a melancholic man like yourself?

—A prostitute? I asked.

—No, he said, pausing for only a second, a new suit.

He pulled a blue jacket off the rack and had me in it before I could protest.

—Ah, he said. A perfect fit. Now try these.

He handed me a pair of pants and, taking hold of my elbow, lead me to a change room.

So I put on the pants.

A sullen and ancient man with a tape measure around his neck and a tailor's chalk in his hand was waiting for me when I stepped out of the change room. He had me step onto a wooden box and, without a word, he took to measuring my inseam. When he was finished, he wrote some numbers down on a scrap of paper and shuffled into a back room.

Moshe appeared before me, nodding approvingly.

You can't go wrong with this suit, he said. She might even come back once she sees you in it. A trim wouldn't hurt either. He brushed his swollen knuckles along the edge of my beard.

I looked at my reflection in a nearby mirror. It was a better a fit than my bar mitzvah suit. That much was true. And Moshe had a point, a trim wouldn't hurt. I looked ridiculous. My neck, I hadn't seen in months. The skin around my eyes was dark, so dark, and my eyes themselves appeared as if they had seen things they had no business ever seeing. Which was not the case, but still. I looked like a raccoon in a suit.

—How much, I asked?

Moshe smiled and patted me on the back.

—For you, he said, a very special price.

I bought the suit. I wear it every day. I'm wearing it now.

METICULOUS, SAD, AND LONELY

The job ad asked, Are you meticulous, sad and lonely? Check, check and check, said Muriel. She read and re-read the ad several times, underlined key words, highlighted industry-specific terms, circled typos (she found two!), and made notes in the margins. She spent the rest of the afternoon crafting the perfect cover letter and adjusting her resume to reflect each job qualification and requirement listed in the ad. Was she creative and efficient? Yes she was. Could she meet tight deadlines and display good time management? Unquestionably. Was she open to new challenges and willing to learn? Of course she was. Did she have a post-secondary degree in biology and a MLIS? As a matter of fact she did. Familiarity and ease with computers? What year was this? Of course! And could she operate a spectrometer? In her sleep. After three rounds of proofreading the following morning—with fresh eyes!—Muriel sent in her cover letter and resume and waited for the call.

    She got the job! Of course she did. She was the only one who applied. Muriel called her mother and said, You're speaking to the new Client-Generated Foodstuff Discolouration Consultant for the public library! Her mother said, Technically, I wasn't speaking. You just called and blurted that out before I had a chance to say anything. Muriel's mother was like that, but then so was Muriel. Two peas in a pod is what Muriel's dad used to call them. Before he left, of course. After he left—two days before Muriel's fifteenth birthday—he stopped calling them anything at all.

    —Well, congratulations I guess, said Muriel's mother Jean.

Jean was no nonsense; Jean was waiting for a grandchild.

Muriel's new job was to identify and catalogue the food stains that clients left behind in books. Muriel's supervisor, Gail, told Muriel that the previous CGFDC cataloguer had moved on to greener pastures. Gail then leaned in and whispered, She died. Seeing Muriel's worried expression, Gail added, Of natural causes. She assured Muriel that it was very important work. And the backlog alone could keep her busy for years to come.

It didn't occur to Muriel to ask why the library needed a CGFDC; she was just happy to have found a job for which she was perfectly suited. Gail had mentioned something in the interview about a sizable donation from a major player in the food industry that made the position possible. At the time, she pushed a piece of paper across the table to Muriel. It had on it the name of the corporation in question. Muriel read it and looked up at Gail. Gail simply smiled and nodded.

Muriel proved to be very good at her job. She could identify and dismiss non-food stains at a glance. Vaseline, blood, motor oil. These were not part of her mandate. With most food stains, visual clues alone were enough for Muriel. She had a gift—or the gift, as Gail put it. Nine times out of ten, all Muriel needed to look at were the 6 major components of discolouration: tone, hue, chromaticity, saturation, vibrancy and, sometimes, iridescence. Only occasionally would Muriel have to do the Olfactics Test. And on very rare occasions, the dreaded Gustatory Test, which involved carefully scraping off tiny particles directly from the page, mixing them with small amounts of distilled water and then, well, tasting it. You do what you've got to do. That was her motto, her mantra, her M.O..

Muriel's office was in the basement of the library. She had her own miniature laboratory down there. She even had an eye-wash sink! For a while, it worked out quite well. Muriel had a job, a steady income. She could afford a nice apartment, nice clothes. She ate out at least once a week. Guilt free! She went on holiday once a year. During the off-season, but she wasn't complaining.

Muriel always thought that once she had her career in place, once she had a job and a purpose, then everything else would follow. A loving partner, a family. A home. These were things she wanted. And she imagined that they would bring an end to her sadness, an end to her loneliness. But that simply wasn't happening. Her work was going well, sure; she felt fulfilled in that respect. But something was missing. And Muriel had to be honest with herself: she wasn't young anymore. Women her age were already getting divorced, sharing custody with deadbeat dads, marrying up. Muriel decided to work on the loneliness by going out on a few dates. She figured less lonely would mean less sad.

But that went nowhere. Four months in and two dates later, Muriel was exhausted by the whole process. Those guys were dreadful bores. Both of them.

She allowed her mother to set her up with a friend's son. Carl was coming out of a long relationship. Muriel heard all about it. His ex was a bitch who took their cat and wouldn't return Carl's calls. He told Muriel this within five minutes of sitting down.

—Maybe you should get another cat, suggested Muriel.

—I don't even like cats! That's the thing, said Carl, swirling his drink and staring past Muriel. That's the whole thing with her, he said.

Next was a handsome younger man named George. Muriel was intrigued.

—You never meet Georges anymore, she said to her mom. When's the last time you met a George.

—My mechanic is named George.

—Yeah, but he's probably old.

—He's twenty-five.

George was in web applications. Muriel heard all about it. He loved his job. He said, You know those nerdy kids in high school who built their own computers?

—Sure, said Muriel.

—I hated those kids, said George. I beat them up. He punched his right hand into the palm of his left. Now look at me! I'm one of them.

Muriel nodded uncomfortably.

—Thing is, said George, some of those retards work for me. Seeing Muriel flinch, he added, Pardon my French. Do you, like, have a retarded brother?

—No, said Muriel. I just... don't like that word.

George rolled his eyes.

Muriel isn't proud of what she did next. Before the entrées arrived, before she finished her first glass of wine, Muriel excused herself saying she needed to use the restroom. She made her way to the back of the restaurant, walked straight through the kitchen—no one said a thing!—and out the back door of the restaurant into a dirty alley that reeked of garbage and marijuana smoke. She almost texted George the next day to apologize or make some excuse about being sick and having to rush out like that. But she didn't.

It was a few weeks after her date with George that Muriel met Spencer. Spencer worked at the library, too. Where else would she meet a man? An eligible man! Spencer had a brush cut and wore jeans and sandals every day of the week. Even in the winter. Muriel once saw him get off the bus in a snowstorm wearing a parka and a pair of Birkenstocks. He drank coffee from a reusable mug and ate carrot sticks during his morning break. Spencer transferred from another branch. He worked in IT. It was Spencer who helped develop and program the cataloguing system that Muriel used. So he had an intimate knowledge of just what she did and he knew all the right questions to ask. It was Spencer who checked in on Muriel when he had absolutely no obvious reason to do so. No one else went down to her office. Even her supervisor Gail had yet to visit Muriel down there; she chose instead to Instant Message Muriel from her office one floor up. But when Spencer showed up... Oh boy. Muriel would blush and act like a school girl. How long had it been since she felt and acted this way? Too long, that's how long.

  Spencer. She liked saying his name. Spencer, Spencer, Spencer. She'd whisper it while she worked. Spencer. Dijon mustard stain (easy) in a copy of *I'm Okay—You're Okay*. Spencer. '97 Côte de Rhône (stain was, interestingly, shaped like Florida panhandle—she added this note to the comments field), found in a copy of *What To Expect When You're Expecting*—Muriel tried not to judge; everyone deals with things in their own way. Spencer. Milk (with a hint of cinnamon—probably spilled from a bowl of Cinnamon Toast Crunch cereal), found on page 49 of *The Sibley Field Guide to Birds of Eastern North America*. She made a note about the bird found on page 49: The Least Bittern. She joked—to herself—that she was the least bittern person she knew. She wasn't. That was the joke.

The first one she got wrong was an apple sauce stain (page 256 of *Gluten-Free and Loving It!*). She input all the data and forgot about it. It was discovered by the new guy in Client Services. Charles. Charles just happened to be reading the book, he said, and he just happened to come across the stain, and he just happened to look it up on the catalogue, and he just happened to do a taste test (Who does that?), and he just happened to determine that it was not apple sauce at all (Wasn't that obvious? he asked Muriel rhetorically. What with the missing tell-tale acidic cidery smell?), and he just happened to determine that what it was, in fact, was Hollandaise sauce! Like Muriel, Charles was also sad and lonely, but he was also miserable and curmudgeonly. So while Muriel didn't have to worry about him taking her job, she was nonetheless concerned.

  A little while later it was breast milk in a copy of *German for Dummies*—she thought it was almond milk. Charles again. A scotch whiskey stain in a Bukowski book—so obvious; she beat herself up over that one. She thought it was orange juice. Orange juice! My god! She was asleep at the wheel.

The problem was that Muriel was happier now, less lonely. Things were going really well with Spencer. They spent their weekends together, going to the movies, watching sunsets, drinking coffee and eating croissants in bed on Sunday morning. It was like a dream. Or a corny movie. One or two nights a week, Muriel went out for drinks with some of Spencer's colleagues from IT. They laughed at her jokes! One woman even complimented Muriel on the important work she was doing. It was going to her head and her senses were failing her. Well, the ones that paid the bills.

It came as no surprise, then, when Gail gave Muriel an ultimatum: she had to choose between happiness and work.

—That's how it is with this job, Gail said. One or the other. Can't have it both ways.

Muriel chose Spencer. They were going to get married. Or engaged. Someday. She was sure of it.

And everything was fine. For a few of weeks.

Losing her job made Muriel sad. Not sad like before, not like the old Muriel. This was a new kind of sad. She became despondent, lethargic, maybe even resentful. No, definitely resentful. She stopped going out with the IT crew. She told Spencer that it didn't feel right to be hanging out with those people anymore. And on the weekends, well, Muriel said she'd rather stay in and watch foreign films. And no more croissants in bed. She couldn't stand the crumbs left behind in the sheets. Sex? Forget it; she wasn't interested.

Spencer found this new Muriel a bit of a drag. And it wasn't long before he hooked up with a bartender. He didn't even drink, Muriel told her mother. So just how the hell did he meet a bartender?

This made Muriel feel so alone.

So alone. Alone. Lone. Lonely. That old sad and lonely spark was reawakening in Muriel. The way she saw it, she had two options. Let it eat away at her until she was old and alone and working at a job she hated, or let it eat away at her until she was old and alone and working at a job for which she had a gift. Muriel checked online and found that the job ad was back up; the position was unfilled. Of course it was. Her mind was made up. Muriel threw herself into training. She decided that she would do whatever she had to do to get her job back. She borrowed dozens of books from the library and practiced every day. She made a spreadsheet. She turned her kitchen into a laboratory. She took cooking classes to brush up on her culinary knowledge. She walked down to the all night grocery store at one, two in the morning and wandered the aisles, reading the ingredients of everything in the store. She sniffed and tasted whatever she could get her hands on. Muriel was meticulous in the planning and execution of each and every aspect of her training. She had never felt so sad and so lonely in her life; she had never felt so alive.

THE LION AND THE WRITER

Once upon a time there was a writer who went on an African safari. He said he was searching for adventure—as if adventure was lost and it was up to him to find it. Yeah, right. This writer was pretty annoying. Apropos of nothing at all, he'd say things like: Well, Kierkegaard says that anxiety is a necessary element of creativity. And: Without fear, there is no progress, there is no possibility! The other people on the safari were getting pretty tired of this. One by one, they exchanged looks with the guide that said: either he goes or I go.

They decided to leave him behind as soon as they got a chance.

He was inconsiderate, said one of the travelers. His beard smelled funny, said another. He took up a lot of space, said a third traveler, stretching out his legs on the now vacant seat beside him. So off they drove in their seven-seater Land Rover, leaving the writer to fend for himself in the wilds of Africa.

Well, it wasn't long before a lion saw the writer. And the lion thought: Yum, dinner. The lion chased the writer. And because the writer was kind of old and out of shape, it wasn't hard for the lion to catch him. The lion was almost disappointed by this because he was accustomed to having to work a little harder for his meals. But a meal was a meal. The lion bit into the writer's neck with his powerful jaws and his huge teeth and he brought that writer down like a sack of stuffing.

But just as the lion was about to take a bite out of the writer, he smelled the writer's beard. And it smelled like a croissant. It was not in the lion's nature to like croissants. He was not a French a lion. He was an African lion. There was no way he could eat this writer. It pained him to walk away from a kill. He was the kind of lion who liked to use all of his prey. For example, when he first saw the writer cowering behind that patch of tall grass, he considered making a nice little wind chime out of the writer's bones and hanging it outside his den. But he had absolutely no use for that beard. So he left the writer there on the savannah. Let the hyenas have him, the lion thought, they'll eat anything. And off he went to find something good to eat. The end.

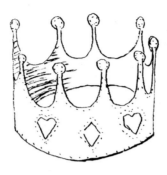

WHEN MOTHER LOVED THE BEAR

When my mother ran off with the bear it made the headlines every day for a week. There was even an alleged photo of the two of them retreating into the woods arm in arm, the bear wearing that stupid plastic crown on his head. I say alleged because it looked like one of those photos people try to pass off as proof of a sasquatch sighting: blurry and unrecognizable. It could have been two porcupines in a tree. The story stayed in the paper for nearly a month. And they reported on every possible, obscene angle they could think of or invent. When they called my father for an interview, he hung up. When they called back, he had the phone disconnected. Eventually the story dropped below the fold, and then on to page two and then three, until some other story came along and replaced it.

    For days afterward, my father left all the windows and doors open. One morning he had me follow him around the house, holding small saucers of dried lavender in my hands and balanced on my forearms like a waiter carrying small plates of exotic and expensive desserts. My father would take one of the saucers and stoop down to place it in a corner or behind a door. He'd then motion for me to follow while walking purposefully across the room to the next corner. My mother had begun carrying the foul, earthy smell of the bear for weeks before she left. But we didn't know then why she smelled like she'd been rolling around in the dirt and possibly in her own feces. We didn't know then that she'd been marked by the bear. There had been clues, signs: the scratches on her back and sides, fur stuck to her clothing and in her hair—but mostly that musky smell. It just never occurred to us.

It was autumn when my father first spotted the bear in the middle of our yard. It was sitting on a thick, low branch in the apple tree. He was eating our apples. My father let the bear remain in the tree until we needed to go out. He then started the car and honked the horn until the bear carefully climbed out of the tree and ambled into the forest. He was in no hurry to leave. And he returned the very next day. But this time he sat on his haunches, eating the rotting apples off the ground. He looked like an overgrown child sitting there under the tree. And again the honking horn, and the ambling off into the forest.

    This whole time my mother refused to go outside. She said she was afraid of the bear. I often found her standing by the window, watching.

    —He's very mysterious, she once said.

    But when I asked what she meant, she turned from the window and asked me what I wanted for supper.

    The bear continued to return to our yard right up until the first snowfall. And then a long, cold winter followed. My mother spent her days reading. Her books piled up on her side of the bed; great, toppling towers of books. And more of them next to the couch in the living room. And scattered throughout the house. She and my father spoke very little. But neither did they argue. Our home was quiet, mostly quiet.

    One evening after I went to bed, I heard music coming from the living room downstairs. My father rarely listened to music, and when he did, it was almost solely Mozart. But my father was already in bed; I could hear him snoring down the hall. I crept down the stairs, and sat on the landing where my mother couldn't see me. She was listening to "Here Comes the Sun." And when the song came to the end, she rose from her chair and crossed the room to the turntable. As the opening notes of "Because" played, she gently lifted the needle, and brought it back to the beginning of "Here comes the Sun." She then returned to her chair, and listened with closed eyes. When the song finished the second time, she crossed the room again and returned the needle to the beginning of the song. She did this over and over. I went back to bed.

There remained a small pile of snow hidden in the shadows of the yard when the bear reappeared that spring. There were no apples, of course, but the tree was already covered with white blossoms. My mother had taken to reading out in the yard. Sometimes I'd look out the kitchen window and see her lips moving, though I could not make out what she was saying. If she caught me watching her, she'd smile or wave and go back to her book.

On one of those afternoons, I came home from riding my bike and my mother was not there. Only her book remained, turned over in the grass under the tree, spread eagle to keep her page. I leaned my bike against the house, and called for her inside. But she wasn't in there. I walked around the yard calling her name. We had a large property, surrounded by a forest on two sides, a lake on one and the road on the other. I walked down the laneway to the road, and looked left and right but she was not there. Back in the yard, I stood at the edge of the forest. A chipmunk scuttled across some leaves; a blue jay screeched in a tree and another answered its call from not too far off. Otherwise, it was quiet. I walked back down into the yard, and sat against the apple tree. I picked up my mother's book. *Wuthering Heights*. I thought the title had been misspelled.

I was on page thirty-four when I heard her coming through the woods. I dropped the book and stood up narrowly against the tree. Without knowing why, or intending to do so, I hid behind the tree and waited for her to pass. I thought of jumping out and startling her. But she walked right by without noticing me and went straight into the house. I expected her to call my name, to come out and look for me. But she didn't. I stood there for sometime before going inside.

My mother had changed her clothes and was making tea in the kitchen. Her hair was tied back in a ponytail.

—There he is, she said too loudly, smiling too broadly.

—Where were you? I asked.

—I went for a lovely walk in the woods.

As she reached across the stove to turn off the kettle, her ponytail fell to the side of her head, exposing a long, deep scratch on the back of her neck.

—What happened to your neck? I asked.

She ran a finger along the length of the scratch. The blood was still wet.

—Oh, I guess I scratched myself on a bramble.

She undid her ponytail and put the elastic in her pocket.

The next morning the bear was in the yard. He had dragged his nails the length of the trunk of the apple tree. Eight long gashes stretching down to the base of the trunk. He had also knocked over our garbage can and rooted through it. When my father got home from work, he honked the horn several times before the bear wandered off. This scene was repeated five days in a row. The bear, the garbage, the tree.

On the fifth day, the bear showed up wearing the plastic crown on his head. He must have found it in someone else's garbage. My father said he was going to call animal control. Perhaps they would trap the bear and relocate it. Or maybe they would shoot the bear.

On the sixth day, my mother left.
She walked out into the yard. And kept walking.
Wuthering Heights was still under the apple tree. The book had been damaged by the rain and sun. It had expanded to nearly double its original thickness.

Almost immediately, there were reports of sightings of the two of them together. And then the photo of my mother and the bear walking into the woods. My father was ridiculed. And I was teased. Even my teacher at school couldn't help herself, calling me a cub, and referring to my hands as paws. My father pulled me out of school, and left me in charge of my own education.

Five mornings a week, my father would wake me at seven, and we'd walk wordlessly down to the lake. My father, carrying a towel and two cups of coffee, would already be dressed for work. He would stand at the shore and watch me toe the water, testing the temperature. I already knew the water was cold; it made no difference.

—There are two kinds of people, my father would say from the shore. Those who wade in slowly and those who dive in bravely. Which are you?

I'd dive in without answering and begin the slow swim across the lake and back.

This was how we began each weekday morning.

I was still unable to make it across and back without stopping to rest. Treading water out in the middle of the lake, my head bobbing just above the surface, I'd watch my father and wonder what he would do if I suddenly went under. I had never seen him swim in my life, and we did not own a boat. I trusted that he had a plan, some way of saving me. But I never asked. Once ashore, he'd hand me the towel and a cup of coffee, and we'd head back up to the house.

After breakfast, my father would leave for the high school where he taught science to bored teenagers. And I would stay home to read and study. My only instructions were to not wander into the forest and to spend at least two hours on my father's directed scientific reading. This involved a high-school science textbook written by my father, and a series of questions and problems about cells and enzymes and proteins and ecology. I was not yet in grade 6.

My own directed reading program involved slowly making my way through my mother's books. Hawthorne, Austen, the Brontës, Dickens. I'd sit under the apple tree in the yard, with a glass of water or—if my father had made any—lemonade, and a pile of my mother's books. My father warned me against only focusing on the soft subjects—this referred to anything that wasn't science. But he did not try to thwart my reading, nor stop me from reading my mother's books.

    I read them not because I was interested in the authors or stories—though I liked Dickens well enough—no, I read them because I thought I might learn something about my mother. At first, I just fanned the pages hoping a note would fall into my lap. I did find some handwritten notes, which were used as bookmarks. A recipe for cinnamon rolls, a grocery list (peppers, fennel, milk, sugar, cereal). One such note appeared to be the beginning of a poem:

> A bird, a bird, landed with wings outspread.
> Dries oil-black feathers in afternoon sun:
> Slight hooked beak, and emotionless eyes red,
> A harbinger, the season has begun.

    I was pleased to immediately recognize this as a cormorant, possibly the double-crested cormorant. I had been tested on my knowledge of cormorants and other migratory birds. And I had seen a few out in the lake. They never stayed very long. Cormorant feathers are not entirely waterproof. That's why they stand with wings outstretched: it's to dry them off. I wondered why a bird that gets its food from lakes and rivers would not have evolved to have waterproof wings? I asked my father; he said, maybe someday it will.

    There was nothing about bears. And of course, no letters or notes explaining why she left.

It wasn't long before summer. And both my father and I were home alone, the two of us struggling to fill our days. I would often find him at the window, staring out into the yard toward the forest. Having decided that we should keep busy, my father began planting a garden: tomatoes, lettuce, basil, and radishes. Pumpkins and squash. Sunflowers and marigolds. When he wasn't tending the garden, he was reading books about tending the garden. We made frequent visits to the public library. At first, my father kept his head down when we ventured into town. But after several weeks of this, he gave up on fake humility—or humiliation. And we strode into the public library, chins up, sometimes chatting and laughing easily. But more often, silent.

    And then summer ended, and autumn began. It was one of those Septembers that make up for a lousy summer. The sun shone almost everyday, and what little rain that fell, fell over night. The leaves on all the trees around the house were still very much green and the flowers we had planted in the spring were still in bloom. But the night air held the cold promise of autumn and the coming winter. And the lake was very, very cold. My father was back at school, and I was back at my directed reading. Although now I was allowed to go to the library on my bicycle, by myself. I was thrilled. On that first visit, I brought home as many books as I could carry. I accidentally dropped some of them in the mud left behind by an overnight rain. After that, I was allowed no more than three books at a time. It only meant more library visits.

October began, and the weather changed. The temperature dropped and snow fell early, petrifying the leaves on all the trees. The apples fell, almost over night. My father raked them up, enough to fill a garbage can. He left them by the road to be picked up with the trash. One morning I woke up to find a thin layer of ice spreading out from the shore, almost to the centre of the lake. And although the ice melted by noon, there would be no more swimming in the mornings, and for that I was thankful. Without the swimming, our routine was almost unchanged. My father still woke me early, only now I was to run the length of the laneway and back, six times. He calculated that this was the equivalent of one kilometre. His concern was that my bookish nature would leave me at a great disadvantage in the world.

Not long after the last red leaf fell from the apple tree, my mother pushed her way through the forest and into our yard. Her clothes hung loose and torn on her thin body. Her hair was matted and wild; her face, dirty and stained. She looked beat, uncared for. Except for her eyes. They were fiercely alive. And so different from how I remembered them. My father was the first to hear her approaching, but he only watched from the window. He stood with his arms folded across his chest, staring, expressionless. I ran out the door and across the yard toward her. But when I got close, the smell and sight of her overwhelmed me and I barely had time to turn my head before I threw up. My face was wet with tears and snot before I even realized I was crying. I wiped at my face with my sleeve and looked up at my mother. There were tears in her eyes and her arms were outstretched. I allowed her to pull me into her arms.

It felt good to be in my mother's arms again. I held my breath and tried to savour it. But when I looked up into her dirty, wild face, I felt I was looking at a stranger. I broke free from her grasp and backed away toward the house. I knew this woman was my mother, I knew she loved me, but she was no longer the mother who left in the spring. I ran inside the house and my father closed the door behind me. Upstairs from my bedroom window, through my own tears, I watched my mother cry in our yard. She stared at the living room window, where my father must have been standing, and she began to undress. She left her clothes in a dirty, foul pile looking like so many fallen leaves. She then walked toward the lake, and kept walking right in to the water until it was over her head. She broke the surface moments later, and swam and scrubbed at her body. I watched from my bedroom window as my father emerged from the house carrying a towel and a bar of soap. He approached the shoreline and tossed the soap to my mother. It landed a few feet from her and floated on the surface. She reached out and began lathering herself. I watched as my father stood there, with the towel in his hand, waiting for my mother to emerge from the water.

THE FUNERAL

They told me that when grandpa died he flew up to heaven to be with the angels. I said, That's bullshit, he didn't even have wings. And my mom said, That's no way for a six year-old boy to talk. And then I said, Fuck you.

And I've been in my room ever since.

But that's okay with me because I don't want to be down there anyway, with all the adults pretending to be sad, pretending to care that grandpa died. I heard what my mom said to my aunt Pam: I won't miss him, she said, I can tell you that.

And then what my aunt Pam said: We're all better off. Now we can start the healing.

If I was down there right now, I'd say to Aunt Pam: That sounds like new age bullshit to me, Auntie Pam. You don't know what you're talking about.

But instead I'm up here in my room, talking to a fucking teddy bear.

TONY MACFUCKINGDOUGALL

This one's true. This one happened. I was walking home from the liquor store, a small bottle of Fireball Whisky tucked into my inside coat pocket, thinking about this and that. Mostly I was thinking about this woman I wanted to sleep with. Sorry to be so blunt—but I need to be honest here. I made a new year's resolution. That's partly what this is about. It was winter, cold but tolerable. That's not always the case here. Sometimes it gets so cold that I call in sick at work because I can't bear to leave the house. I also hate my job. So much honesty in one short paragraph. I work for Statistics Canada. I work with numbers. And I hate numbers.

So I was walking and thinking, thinking and walking. Every now and then I'd pull my phone out of my pocket and listen. The other end of the line was quiet. Good, that meant the kids were still asleep. This woman I was thinking about is married. She has kids. Two of them, same as me. I started making a habit of being places where I knew I'd see her. The Y on Sunday morning for the kids' swim, a certain fast food chain on Fridays—she takes the kids there after work. It got to the point where we both knew it was no longer a coincidence that I was showing up. But she didn't tell me to cut it out or back off. In fact, last time it happened, she said, I'll see you here next week! And then she smiled—in a way that I thought was a little flirty. I know she's not happy in her marriage. She has said some things, made some hints. Her name is Blue. Her parents were hippies. I said one time, Do you know that Dylan song, "Tangled up in Blue"? She didn't. I said, What kind of hippies were your parents if you don't know that song? The kind that smoked weed and listened to Jimi Hendrix, she said. Point taken, I said.

There's a part of my walk home that dips beneath the highway. It's dark under there during the day; it's especially dark at night. I usually don't think too much about it. It was walking through there, about to exit the other side, thinking as I was about this woman, Blue, when two guys stepped into the tunnel and blocked my path. One of them was holding a knife.

—Give me your money, said the guy with the knife.

—Are you fucking kidding me? I said.

It was out of my mouth before I knew what I was saying. This is a problem I have, have always had.

—Give me your fucking money now.

—Did Tony put you up to this?

I acted like I was really angry.

—Who the fuck is Tony?

—Who the fuck is Tony? Ha! Now I know that motherfucker is behind this. That piece of shit. Where the fuck is he?

My voice was getting loud. I started looking around, over their shoulders for Tony.

—What the fuck are you talking about? asked the other guy, the guy not holding a knife.

I will admit to using some language here that I don't normally use.

—I know that jesusmotherfuckingchristly piece-of-shit is around here somewhere, I said.

I called over their shoulders: Where the fuck are you, you piece of shit?

I was shouting now, spit was flying out of my mouth. I was also conscious of not yelling too loud. I didn't want to wake up the kids.

Guy with the knife: Empty your pockets and shut the fuck up!

Me: You tell that sonuvabitch to come out here where I can fucking see him.

I started yelling over their heads again: You think you can fucking scare me? You're the guy who raped my little sister, you piece of shit. Come out here right fucking now.

—Whoa! What the fuck are you talking about?

—I know Tony sent you guys. I'm not fucking stupid.

—We don't know Tony.

—Tony. You don't know Tony? Holy fuck, how stupid do I look?

—Tony who? This is the guy not holding the knife. And he asks kind of tentatively.

The guy with the knife nudges him, but he looks at me, waiting for an answer.

—Tony who? Tony Mac. And then I shout past them: Tony Mac, you piece of shit. Everybody knows it's MacFuckingDougall.

And then quieter, to the two guys: Wants everyone to think he's Italian. Piece of shit is more Scottish than fucking bagpipes. Tony Mac, my ass. Where is he? I swear to god I'll fucking cut him in two.

—What is your beef with Tony Mac?

—What's my beef? Because you don't know, right? Because he didn't tell you before he put you up to this? He probably told you I took something from him? That piece of shit slept with my little sister. She's sixteen years old and he's a fucking grown man. That's statutory rape. So my brother and I let people know we were looking for him. Next thing I know, he fucking threatens my sister. Says for her to keep her mouth shut or else. After what he did, he threatens her? Really? What kind of man is that? Then I hear that he's looking for me because, and I quote, he wants to fuck me up. Fuck me up? No, Tony Mac. You do not do what you did to my little sister and then fuck me up. That is not how it fucking works.

—I'm telling you, bud, we don't know Tony Mac.

—I want to fucking believe you—you look like good guys—but this has Tony Mac written all over it. Too chicken shit to come out here like a fucking man. He has to send you two—like I said, you look like good guys. But you shouldn't work for that piece of shit.

—We don't know Tony Mac, pal. But if we did, I'd hold him down and let you take a few swings at him because he sounds like a piece of shit.

—I have a little sister, too, says the other guy.

And we're all quiet for just a second.

—Tony Mac is a piece of shit. If you see him, tell him I want to have a word with him. I want to have a word and then kick his ass.

And then I walk away. And I don't look back.

I broke into a sprint when I got around the first corner. My feet hardly touched the ground. I pulled my phone out and listened. Still quiet at the other end. I ran all the way to my street, up the stairs and into my building. I put the chain on the door inside my apartment for the first time since forever. The kids were both still sound asleep. I took the phone from next to their bed and hung it up. And then turned off my cell phone. I call it the poor man's baby monitor.

I closed their bedroom door and laughed the laugh of a very lucky man. Almost took a bow. I really couldn't believe it. That performance deserved a drink. I took the bottle of whiskey out of my pocket and took a long pull on it. A few deep breaths.

I did a bit of acting in high school. I wasn't bad. Grease. I did Grease one year.

There was no Tony Mac. Well, there was a long time ago. A kid I went to elementary school with. Nice kid. Kind of strange. One time he came running into the bathroom at school, yelling and scratching at himself. Ants, he screamed, ants all over me. And he proceeded to tear off all his clothes in the middle of the bathroom. Stripped right down to nothing while rolling around on the floor. And sure enough, all these ants came streaming out of the pile of clothes on the concrete floor, looking for some place to go. I'll never forget that. I just stood there at the urinal, looking at this naked kid rolling around on the floor, scared out of his mind because of some ants. I zipped up and walked out without saying a word to Tony MacDougall. We never spoke about it. I never told anyone. I wonder what happened to that kid.

Once I'd calmed down a bit, I got a glass and poured myself a generous amount of whiskey. I couldn't believe that I pulled that off. I almost dialled the ex, to tell her about those guys and what I did. That still happened a lot: that impulse to call her whenever anything interesting happened. I guess it's normal; we were together for a few years. She'd probably say I was an idiot and I could've gotten myself killed. She'd also be awfully curious as to why I wasn't home with the kids. Best not to be the one to start that conversation. I thought about calling Blue but I didn't have her number. Yet. That would come. And go.

A noise from the bedroom. One of the kids was stirring. I let out a long breath and my feet touched back down on the floor. My ex would have been right: I could have gotten myself killed. And then what? I had a driving instructor years ago who warned me that if I looked at the ditch by the side of the road, then that's where I'd end up. If you look at the ditch, he'd say, then you're gonna take the ditch. I drank what was left in my glass and went into the bedroom to try and get my son back to sleep.

5 CENTS

The first time it happened, he was a baby: nearly six months old, still breastfeeding, just starting on solid food. His mother found the lump while nursing him. He bit her nipple and giggled. She pulled him off her breast and gently reprimanded him. And that's when she noticed it: a small red welt hidden behind his right ear.

Her first thought was that it was a spider bite. She checked his crib but found no trace of a spider. She got a magnifying glass and inspected the welt, looking for a puncture wound. She wasn't sure if there was such a thing as a puncture wound when it came to spider bites—but it was worth a look. Nothing. She felt the small lump, rolling it around softly under her index finger. The baby winced. She decided to keep an eye on it.

They went to the kitchen for breakfast. Mashed banana for him, coffee for her. The baby's father had gone to work. He worked in an office where he wrote reports and attended meetings. That's what he told people he did and then he'd change the subject.

After breakfast, the welt had grown larger. Now and then the baby would reach behind his ear and scratch at it. The mother covered it with a bandage. By that afternoon, the skin around the bandage was swollen and warm to the touch. She called her husband and described the welt to him over the phone.

—It's angry and red, she said. About the size of my thumb.
—From the first knuckle? He asked.

—The first knuckle? She said. Yeah, I guess.

—Well, is it the one closest to the fingernail or the one next to the valley between the index finger and the thumb?

—Closest to the fingernail.

—Oh, he said. Okay. Maybe it's an ear infection.

—It's behind his ear. Not in it. I'm rolling my eyes right now, she said, in case you can't hear that in my voice.

—Hmm.

She could hear him tapping away at his typewriter.

—Are you typing while you talk to me?

—I'm... no.

—I see.

—If it gets bigger, bring him to the ER.

That afternoon, it got bigger.

She got the baby ready and put him in the car. As she was strapping him into the seat, the belt rubbed against the welt and he screamed.

—Sorry, she said.

The baby scrunched up his face. She really felt terrible about this; she felt responsible—like she had done something to cause the welt. She kissed the baby's ear and then again just above the bandage covering the welt. The baby napped during the drive to the hospital. Now and then, he'd whimper in his sleep. It reminded her of a dog she used to have. He slept at the foot of her bed and often woke her in the night with his whimpering and quiet, dreamy yips. This was before the baby, before her husband. Back when she was alone and had a different idea of the person she would become.

They waited for over an hour before a doctor saw them. By that time, the welt had swollen so much that the bandage was touching the back of the baby's earlobe.

A nurse led them into a small room. The mother sat with the baby on her lap and sang "Twinkle, Twinkle Little Star." She blushed when the doctor entered the room and caught her singing. He looked about twelve years old. That didn't help.

—What seems to be the problem? He asked.

She explained.

He walked over to the baby and smiled. He felt around the baby's neck and listened to the baby's heart and looked in the baby's ears. He tapped on the baby's back and looked in the baby's mouth and peered deep into the baby's eyes and then made a face to make the baby laugh. It was while the baby was laughing that the doctor quickly peeled off the bandage. The baby was startled but didn't cry. Upon seeing the welt, the doctor sucked in his breath.

—There appears to be a nickel in your child's... well, in your child.

The mother looked down at the welt. It now held the distinct imprint of a nickel. In curved letters she read 5 CENTS and beneath that, CANADA. And sitting on a log suspended between these words, a beaver.

—That wasn't there this morning, the mother said.

—No, I suppose you would have mentioned it before now.

—How did it get there? The mother asked.

—I don't have a clue.

The mother sensed accusation in his voice.

—Well, I didn't put it there, she said.

She hoped that was obvious.

The doctor brought his face close to the baby's welt. He pressed at it with his finger. The baby cringed and shrieked. The doctor continued to move the lump around a little from side to side. He pushed it. He tapped it.

He stood up, wiped his hands on his lab coat and looked at the mother.

—There is definitely a nickel under there, he said.

—That's impossible, said the mother.

—You would think so, said the doctor. I'll be right back.

The mother held the baby close and looked at the imprint of the nickel in his neck.

—This doesn't make any sense, she said.

The baby made a cooing sound and tugged on the mother's hair.

The doctor returned with two more doctors in tow. One of them was carrying a Polaroid camera. All three crowded around the baby. The first doctor pointed out the welt and said, Behold! The other two rolled their eyes but were visibly impressed.

The doctor with the camera said to the mother, Do you mind? And then, without waiting for an answer, he proceeded to take a picture of the imprint on the baby's neck.

The camera snapped and whirred and a photo emerged from the front of the camera.

The three doctors hovered over the developing image.

—Fascinating, said the first doctor.

—Amazing technology, said the second doctor. He removed the photograph and began fanning it through the air.

The third doctor was unimpressed. She made a little hunh sound and looked at the baby.

The mother cleared her throat.

—Can you please tell me what is going on with my baby?

—We have no idea, said the first doctor.

—This is very unusual, said the third doctor. We'd need to take a

43

look inside to see what we're dealing with. If it's an actual nickel in there... well maybe the little fellow swallowed it.

—But how did it get behind his ear?

—Mystery of the human body, said the second doctor, still fanning the Polaroid photo back and forth.

Two nurses showed up to have a look. And then four more doctors and an orderly. The room was getting very crowded.

—Wow, said the orderly.

—That's not something you see every day, is it?

One of the nurses patted the baby on the head and said, A nickel for your thoughts?

This got a laugh.

The baby buried his face in the folds of his mother's sweater.

Once the Polaroid photograph was developed, it got passed around the room. There was a great deal of humming and head scratching. After some time of this, the doctors and nurses and the orderly were all called away to other patients. And the mother and the baby were left with the original doctor.

—Here's what I'm going to do, the doctor said.

He put on latex gloves, snapping each one a little too dramatically for the mother's taste. She waited for him to finish his sentence.

She cleared her throat.

—I'm going to remove the nickel. And then we'll be done with it. You can put this behind you.

The mother narrowed her eyes but said nothing.

The doctor administered a local anesthetic behind the baby's ear and retrieved a scalpel from his arsenal of tools. The scalpel blade caught the sunlight coming in through the window and the mother held her breath. The baby moaned quietly as the doctor made a small incision. Using his thumb and index finger, the doctor nudged the bloody nickel out of the incision in the baby's skin and dropped it into a kidney-shaped metal pan. He quickly and deftly sewed up the incision with three small stitches. Once that was done, he turned his attention back to the nickel. He cleaned and sterilized it in the sink, all the while humming a tune the mother recognized as the same song she had been singing when he first entered the room.

The doctor stopped humming and walked over to the baby. He made a little flourish with his hand next to the baby's head and pretended to pull the nickel out of the baby's ear like a magician.

—Tada!

He handed the nickel to the mother and smiled. She didn't know what to do with it, so she held it in her closed fist.

—Maybe he'll grow up to be a magician, said the doctor.

But he didn't. He grew up to be an ordinary man who, every year or two, finds a nickel just under the skin behind his ear. Always the right side. There is no predictability to it, no warning. Every now and then, he simply wakes up to find a new welt behind his ear—much like that first time when he was a baby. The doctors stopped being surprised long ago. They remove the nickel, make the same magician joke, and send him on his way. He used to bring the nickels home from the hospital, clean and sterilized, and drop them into a jar on his dresser. He was saving up for a boat. But he doesn't do that anymore. Now he tosses them into the fountain outside the hospital. Each time a coin leaves his hand, he closes his eyes and makes a wish. And it's always the same wish: that these goddamn nickels stop appearing under his skin.

HERE'S THE KICKER

It was something he said all the time. It's how he ended almost every story. I'm in line at the grocery store, right. Long line. I mean, lonnng. And here's the kicker: guy in front of me has a goddamn heart attack. I end up leaving without my can of cream corn and box of Oreos. Or, Turns out I don't have cancer after all. But here's the kicker, I have to get my wisdom teeth removed in a week.

In fact, he did have cancer. Of the spine. And it was pretty advanced. Too late for surgery, too late for alternative remedies in California. He died within 3 months of being diagnosed.

Now every time I hear someone say here's the kicker, I get impatient, I rush them toward the punchline. What? What's the kicker? What is it? Tell me! Tell me now before it's too late.

LUKE AND PEARL AND JONAS AND FIFTY

Luke and Pearl heard Jonas let out a low whistle from the room down the hall. This was his way of informing them that he could hear what they were saying. It was also his way of letting them know that they were interrupting his TV show. Jonas had exceptional hearing. Even when Luke and Pearl were whispering in the shower with the water running, Jonas still heard. He also had a very powerful sense of smell, and could identify the scent of the shampoo they were using while in the shower. Since he'd been living with them, he banned most fragrances from the house. Especially Ylang Ylang: he said it brought back bad memories of the commune.

    The thing about Luke's uncle Jonas was that he was born with the head of an elephant. The family acted as if this were normal. He was born that way, they said, as if that alone were enough of an explanation. Pearl felt otherwise. But what could she say? The man had an elephant head, for God's sake. Describing him over the phone to her sister in Vancouver, Pearl said, No, not like Joseph Merrick. He has actual tusks and a trunk. Like Ganesha. But with all these tattoos on his arms and torso.

    That was six months ago.

    Jonas had called Luke to ask if he could stay at their place for a few days. He explained that he'd had an accident and couldn't get up the stairs to his own apartment; everyone else he knew lived in what he called 'multi-level abodes.' Luke and Pearl lived in a bungalow. As soon as Luke said yes, the doorbell rang.

Jonas was sitting there in a wheelchair with both of his legs wrapped in thick plaster casts. He wouldn't tell Luke and Pearl how he broke his legs; he just said there'd been an accident. Standing behind him, with her hands on his shoulders, was a beautiful young woman with muscular arms. Jonas introduced her as his personal assistant Ilsa. She nodded hello, and then effortlessly rolled Jonas up the front step and into the house. Once inside, Ilsa proceeded to sign both of Jonas's casts simultaneously with two black markers.

—Will you get a load of that, Jonas asked?

When she was done, Ilsa kissed him on the cheek and left without a word.

Jonas's dog Fifty showed up sometime later. On his own. Carrying that day's newspaper between his teeth. Jonas patted the dog on the head and took the paper.

—Will you get a load of that, he asked again?

Pearl had never met Jonas before that day. She'd heard enough about him—the twenty-two months he'd spent in his mother's womb, the small chalky tusks that fell off to make way for his adult tusks—but she thought Luke was exaggerating. She assumed those pictures he showed her had been tampered with somehow. So she was pretty surprised when Jonas showed up at their door, with his wrinkled elephant trunk reaching all the way down to his lap, and his long, curved tusks pointing in opposite directions. Pearl expected him to be… different somehow. Not so outgoing, perhaps. She thought maybe he'd be a little simple or unable to speak as normal people do. But he could speak just fine. He had a lisp that was only apparent after he'd been drinking. Which was often. And when he laughed he made a trumpet-like sound familiar to those who've spent any time around an elephant. Apart from his elephant head, the rest of Jonas's body was quite normal. Two arms, two legs. Even his skin was normal. Just the skin on his head and ears and trunk was a little thicker, a little greyer than the rest. His tattoos, he had several scattered all over his body, looked like he'd done them himself, or had them done in prison. Both of which were true. Although some had been done by professionals.

When he showed up that day, Jonas told them he'd only be staying for a short time. Until a ground-level suite became available in his building, he explained. By the end of the second week, he had most of his belongings dropped off by various friends and acquaintances. A woman on a Harley-Davidson dropped off a duffel bag carrying all of his clothes. She also brought him a pan of hash brownies. The two of them spent the afternoon in Jonas' room, giggling and then making low grunts and moans. Pearl was mortified; Luke turned up the stereo.

The next day two men arrived in a van: they dropped off nearly twenty cardboard boxes. Luke had them pile the boxes up against a wall in Jonas's room. They made another trip the following afternoon. As did the woman on the Harley. A new woman showed up a few times a week after that. Luke and Pearl had no idea where they were coming from, nor how they were able to find Jonas. But find him they did. Pearl was sure they were prostitutes and this upset her a great deal. Luke said he thought they seemed friendly. He'd sometimes make tea or coffee for the women after Jonas had fallen asleep; then he'd see them out, inviting them back anytime they wished.

As the days turned into weeks and then months, Jonas finally admitted that he had actually been evicted from his apartment. There was no ground-level suite. Not for him, anyway.

—So, I'm going to need to crash here until I can walk again, he said.

Luke said, Sure.

Pearl said, We have to talk.

Luke followed Pearl into the kitchen. She popped two pills into her mouth and swallowed a mouthful of water. As they were standing there, Fifty walked in and tugged open the fridge using the dish towel Jonas had Luke tie to the handle. He nosed around in the fridge until he found what he was looking for: a bottle of beer wrapped in a neoprene sleeve. He took it between his teeth, closed the fridge door with his forepaw, and walked out of the room. They could soon hear Jonas praising the dog.

—There's a good boy. Bring that to daddy and I'll give you a sip.

Pearl shook her head and gave Luke one of those looks she'd been giving him since Jonas arrived: clenched teeth, piercing eyes, head shot forward for just a second. Luke shrugged. They really couldn't talk with Jonas in the house.

—Outside. Now.

Pearl's voice sounded forced and unnatural. They stepped out into the backyard.

—He can't stay here any longer. I need him to leave. We. Need. Him. To. Leave.

—He's got nowhere else to go.

—I don't care, Luke. I can't take it anymore.

—What do you want me to do? Put him out on the street?

—Anything. Tell him to go live with his ambidextrous girlfriend.

—She lives in a walk-up, said Luke.

—Send him to the zoo.

Luke gasped. Pearl put her hand over her mouth.

—I can't believe you said that, Luke said.

Pearl took a deep breath.

—He groped me, Luke. He put his hand up my skirt and he groped me.

—Maybe it was an accident.

She turned on him furiously.

—An accident?

Luke sat down on the grass.

—When did this happen? Why didn't you tell me?

—I'm telling you now, Luke. I can't spend another day with him in this house. If he's not gone when I get back, I'm leaving.

Pearl turned and walked out of the yard through the side gate. Luke remained sitting on the grass. He couldn't believe that his uncle would do that. He must have been drunk. Or stoned. Jonas crossed a lot of lines—but that? And after everything they had done for him? Maybe he had been asleep at the time. Maybe it was all a misunderstanding.

His uncle had had a difficult life. There was no denying that. It's true, he was hard to live with. And demanding as all hell since his stint as the leader of that love commune. He became accustomed to people waiting on him, and doing whatever he told them to do. But still, it's not easy going through life with the head of an elephant. Some terrible things happened to Jonas when he was young. Terrible things. Scientific studies, all the shuffling around between labs and experts and people who claimed they wanted to help—but really only wanted to exploit Jonas. And the past few years had been rough on him. He was getting older. And then this thing with the broken legs… Luke felt like he had no choice but to help his uncle. When Luke's father left when Luke was nine, Jonas stepped in and helped out. He took Luke fishing and camping. He taught Luke how to ride a bicycle, how to shoot a rifle, and later, how to roll a joint. It was Jonas who secretly bought Luke a subscription to Playboy when Luke turned thirteen. The man once threatened to gore a kid with his tusks after Luke was bullied at school. He was there for Luke when Luke most needed him.

Fifty scratched at the back door to get out. Luke got up and opened the door for the dog. Fifty walked over to the clothesline and reached with his open mouth for one of Jonas's shirts. The blue shirt he was trying to get was just out of reach, so he settled for the green one next to it. He gently tugged it off the line, and brought it inside the house.

Luke soon heard Jonas scolding the dog.

—Not green, you idiot. I said blue.

Before long Fifty was back in the yard, on his hind legs, reaching for the blue shirt again. Luke went over and took it off the line and handed it to him. Fifty took it, and with his head down, walked back inside. Luke followed the dog in, and put on some coffee. He leaned against the counter and closed his eyes.

    Shortly after he and Pearl started dating, Pearl had all four of her wisdom teeth removed. Luke picked her up from the dentist's office and drove her back to his place. She said strange and wonderful things while coming off the general anesthetic. And Luke couldn't have loved her more. He got her home and into bed where she spent all of the next day recovering. Luke replaced the blood-soaked cotton swabs in her mouth, and made sure she had enough pain medication in her so that she didn't feel a thing. Once it was okay to do so, he fed her Jell-O and pudding and ice cream in bed. It was one of his happiest memories of Pearl. He didn't want her to leave. Not like this.

    —Do I smell coffee? Jonas called.

Luke opened his eyes.

    —Yes. Do you want some?

    —Sure do.

He filled a cup and brought it to his uncle. Jonas was lying in bed, watching a soap opera. A woman was removing her blouse to reveal a lacy bra. A tanned and handsome man was watching her with a lecherous grin. Jonas smiled and took a sip of coffee.

    —A little weak but not bad, he said.

    —I have to talk to you about something, said Luke.

Jonas raised a finger and shushed Luke.

    —Just a sec.

When the show cut to a commercial, Jonas turned and looked up at Luke.

    —Before you start, I just want to say I heard what Judge Judy said out there. And for the record, that's ridiculous. The allegations she made are deeply hurtful to me. You know I would never do something like that to you. I mean, are you kidding me? Pearl? Forgive me for saying this, but she's gotten a bit on the heavy side since I've been here. And yes, I heard that crack about the zoo. It's not like I haven't heard that one before.

Luke bit his lower lip.

    —You've got to go, Uncle Jonas.

    —Buddy, are you going let that woman control every decision you make in life? You've got to be a man here. I see how things are. She's got you whipped. For crying out loud, she's even got you sitting down when you take a piss. It's time to stand up for yourself. Take control. This is your house, too.

    —I know but–

    —Here's the thing, Buddy. I'm going to get that fibreglass cast on my other leg soon, and maybe then I can think about finding a place. But right now, it's just not realistic.

Jonas reached down and patted Fifty on the back. The dog slunk his head down to the floor and glanced up at Luke.

—Yeah, but...

Jonas shook his head, his trunk gently swayed from side to side. He scratched at his armpit and sighed heavily.

—Buddy, Jonas said, there are two kinds of people in this world: Those you can live with, and those you can't live with. Don't get me wrong, I like Pearl. But she is most definitely the former. That woman is impossible. She's a domineering, controlling—excuse my French—bitch.

Luke sighed.

—She's finding it really hard to have you here.

—She's finding it hard? This isn't exactly the Ritz-Carlton. I mean, I appreciate your hospitality. I really do. But this is not ideal for me either, Buddy.

—We need to find you some other place to go, Uncle Jonas.

Jonas smoothed out his trunk.

—The point I'm trying to make here, Buddy, is you can do better. Trust me. Thing is, we're family. Who's she? I don't know her. You know what I mean?

—We've been together for five years.

—She has bad taste in music, Buddy. That right there says a lot about a woman.

Luke pressed on.

—What about Uncle Marty? Could you stay with him for a little while?

—In Scarborough? Are you kidding me? Besides, the point is moot. I've burned some bridges, Buddy. And that's on me. I'll own that. One hundred percent. Uncle Marty. Your mother. My ex. Excuse me, exes. There's no one else, Buddy. You're all I've got.

Luke said nothing.

—You know I've always loved you like the son I never had. Well, that's not entirely accurate. But the sentiment is accurate. And I knew that when the time came, I could count on you. We're family, you and me. That's worth something.

—But about this thing Pearl said you did...

—Simply not true. A misunderstanding. I was reaching for the remote.

The commercial break was over. Jonas winked at Luke and turned his attention back to the soap opera.

—If it'll make her happy, tell her I'll start looking for a place when I get the fibreglass cast.

Fifty raised his head off the floor to watch Luke walk out of the room.

When Pearl got home that night, she took one look at Luke and shook her head. Her expression was inscrutable; there was no flicker of anger or sadness or disappointment. Without a word, she went into their room and started filling a suitcase with clothes.

—I'm going to my mother's house.

—He said he'd go as soon as he—

—I can't stay here.

—You don't have to do this. We can figure something out.

Luke was whispering. Pearl was not.

—He assaulted me. That… thing in there assaulted me. I put up with him because he's your uncle. If he's not leaving, then I will.

—Those are strong words, missy, Jonas called from the other room.

Pearl glared at Luke.

—You are choosing him over me. That is what's happening here. His word over mine.

—She's a liar, Buddy. Didn't I tell you?

—Please stay out of this, Uncle Jonas.

Pearl picked up her suitcase and carried it to the door.

—I don't know if I can forgive you for this.

—I'll get him out, Luke whispered. I'll get him out and then you can come back.

Pearl didn't say anything.

Luke watched her walk down the driveway and get into the car. He could hear his uncle clearing his throat in the other room.

Pearl was backing the car out of the driveway.

Luke opened the door and called out to her.

—Wait, he said, I want to come with you.

But Pearl didn't hear him. Or pretended not to hear him. Luke stepped outside in his socks and turned to close the door behind him. But when he turned back around, she was already gone.

Back inside, Jonas called Luke into his room. He reached out his hand and took hold of Luke's arm.

—You know what I think would make you feel better? Some chicken nuggets. And some of that plum sauce we like so much. What do you say, bachelor?

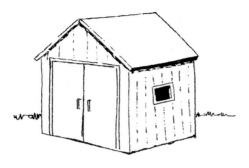

HER NAME IS JANUARY

I opened the door and he punched me in the face. That was a first for me. I had never been punched in the face in my own doorway before. Or anywhere, for that matter. And I'm not ashamed to tell you that I fell right on my ass. I sat there for a while, massaging my jaw and shifting it from side to side. I was happy he didn't break my nose or give me a black eye. And there was no blood: that was good, too. But man, did it hurt. I looked up at him, looking down at me, and I asked if I could buy him a coffee. He told me to fuck off, but offered me his hand all the same. I took it and got back on my feet.

—Jesus, I said. That really hurt.
—Yeah, it was meant to.
—But, shit. I mean, it looks like nothing when they do it on TV.
—Yeah, well, that's TV, asshole.
—I'm sorry about all this, I said. Jan and I… we were both pretty drunk and–
—Her name is January.

I thought he was going to punch me again and I backed off a little. But he turned and walked away. By the way he carried himself and declined my offer to buy him a coffee, I could tell he was enjoying himself, just a little. I mean, he had me at a real disadvantage. I thought I should call after him; something like It was all a misunderstanding or It's not what you think, but it was obviously too late for that. I watched him walk across the street, up the walkway and into his and Jan's house.

There was a neighbourhood party the night before. All the couples, all the kids. There was drinking. Some of the guys lit up behind a shed, like when we were teenagers. Jan—January had been mixing cocktails on her front lawn all evening. And we were wasted. Not Slugger, though: he doesn't drink. That was part of the problem.

Jan and I were talking and flirting. It started out pretty innocent. You know, it always does. But at one point, she put her hand on my arm, and it was like she sent me a message without words. Does that make sense? It sounds stupid but it was like a little benign electric shock running up my arm. After the guys were all gone from behind the shed, Jan and I headed back there and fooled around a bit, nothing serious. She wouldn't even let me put my hand up her shirt. Like I said, it was like when we were teenagers. Only when we were teenagers, the husband didn't show up unexpected, with his dick hanging out ready to take a piss, only to find his wife sticking her tongue down your throat.

THIS IS WHAT HAPPENED WHEN I DIED

The waiting room is enormous, hundreds of seats, nearly all of them occupied, but it's incredibly quiet. No one speaks, no one says a word. But it's not creepy or unnerving. It just is. Also, there's this: the scent of vanilla! It's ingenious, really. I imagine some celestial focus group spent an eternity coming up with the idea. A drop of vanilla essence in the centre of the room creates a remarkably tranquil atmosphere. Try it at home while you still can.

It occurs to me now that the smell might be different for everyone. I'll have to look into that.

Back to the waiting room. It's not like the waiting you're familiar with. No one is impatient, no one is looking at his watch, no one is tapping her fingers on her chair nervously. There is none of that. No, instead, well, think of it like this. You have been brushing and flossing confidently all year, you know with certainty that you do not have a single cavity, there is no tartar build up at all, your gums are in top shape, and you are waiting at the dentist's office—sure, there is some anxiety, some anticipation, but you know it'll be a breeze. In and out without a drop of blood, as the saying goes. It's a little like that.

Eventually, my name was called. Well, okay it wasn't called exactly. It was insinuated. Or implied. Or it was communicated. Look, there's no word for it. I just knew when it was my turn. Okay?

When my name was called, I made my way to the front of the room—there are walls of windows on three sides; the light is… is… it's amazing, actually. You can almost touch it. Seriously—it's like feeling a warm-ish breeze rush over fingers when you reach out into that light. I made my way to the front of the room and through a doorway. A man with thick, bushy sideburns met me there. We didn't shake hands. I thought he might hug me but he didn't. He even said, I'm not going to hug you. But friendly-like, maybe he shrugged a little when he said it. I followed him through an open office with cubicles. There were cubicles in there! Everything was white. There were no computers, no telephones. Just papers and pens and pencils and, curiously, calculators. This was never explained to me and for reasons that will soon become clear, I didn't want to waste my question asking about the calculators.

The man with sideburns led me into his cubicle and motioned to a chair. He sat down across from me.

You get a question, he said. A question about anything. Something you've always wanted to know, something about you or someone else. Had a guy in here yesterday who wanted to know about what really happened to JFK. I told him. A woman the other day asked if there's 'a god', her words. That was a tough one. But a deal's a deal. I told her. One question. What'll it be?

I can only ask one question?

Are you sure you want that to be your question?

Oh shit! Sorry. Oh, no. Can I take it back?

Yes. You would not believe how many times that happens. And that was another question.

It's just that one question doesn't seem like a lot. I mean, that's it. One question. After everything we go through in life, that's all we get.

I was trying hard not to end my sentences with question marks.

That's all you get, you say? Listen—he looked at the sheet on his desk—Richard, Rick: life is what you get. Life is a beautiful thing. You are lucky to get life: to live, to be a human being on planet earth and to feel feelings, do things, make things. To love and suffer and move your body, to be a part of the goddamn world. That's fucking incredible.

Are you allowed to swear?

If I answer that, that will be your one question. I'm not warning you again.

Sorry. Never mind. Geez.

So this one question: it's a gift. This is our way of saying thanks for playing. Sorry you had to die—but wasn't it worth it?

He was quiet for a while. He let that sink in.

Can I have a minute to think?

He tilted his head to the side and looked at me. He wasn't smiling.

Are you kidding me?
Sorry. I'm going to take a minute to think about this.
Take all the time you want.
I closed my eyes for two, three minutes.
And then I asked my question: ███████████████
███████, he said ███████████████████████████
██
██

He told me it was like making a wish when blowing out your birthday candles. Don't tell anyone. Who would I tell, I asked him? He just gave me one of his looks.

And now I'm on a bus.

I'm not sure where it's taking me. The man with sideburns said it would be a lovely place, that I would be happy there. The bus driver—there is a bus driver—has short white hair and wears a cap and a blue uniform. He looks like the doctor in the OR. He smiles as he drives. Now and then he looks back at us—there are several of us on the bus—and he smiles some more. The streets are empty but not eerie. The same light, the same warmth. More buildings, more grass. More trees. We drive on. There is no traffic, no pedestrians. We cross a bridge that spans a lazy, slow moving river. And we keep driving. I used to love riding buses when I was young.

I get up from my seat and make my way to the driver. He looks up at me and smiles.

Good day, he says.

Where are we going, I ask? Where are you taking us?

He smiles, and points in front of us. I look through the cleanest windshield I have ever seen, and I see... what? The road, some buildings. The horizon. I stand there a bit longer, waiting for understanding to kick in.

I don't get it, I say.

You will.

I return to my seat at the back of the bus. And after a while—how long? A minute? An hour? A month?—I think maybe I do get it. But it would be hard for me to explain it to you. It's just something you'll have to see for yourself. Try and think of a good question, though. Have one ready. Then you can get on the bus sooner.

THERE'S A LITTLE BLACK SPOT

He stared at it for a long time, not at all sure what he was looking at. He rubbed his eyes and blinked. He looked away and then back again. But it was still there: a black spot in the otherwise clear blue sky. His first thought was that it was a speck of dust on his cornea. He hit himself on the side of the head a few times to knock it out. But that did nothing but hurt his head and make people look at him funny. The spot remained. It reminded him of a squash ball, if held at double-arm's length. There was a time he played squash, but that was long ago. Well there it is, he thought, another sign that I'm getting old.

Dave was sitting outside on his fifteen-minute coffee break, eating a bran muffin and staring at what—for all he knew—was a hole in the sky. He laughed at the notion—a hole in the sky! That was absurd. Was it even possible? He thought not. He remembered hearing about holes in the ozone layer—how long ago was that? The '90s? Hadn't they fixed that problem? And besides, you couldn't actually see those holes: no, it was like the idea of holes. He would ask the next person who walked by.

—Excuse me. Do you see that? He pointed up. That… that spot?

It was a boy—well, a young man. He was wearing shorts and a baseball cap. Dave would not be caught dead in shorts and a baseball cap. At least not in the downtown core. Those days were long gone.

—Yeah, the kid said, now that you mention it. It's like the shadow of the moon or something. It's a… what do you call that?

—An eclipse, said Dave.
—Yeah. That.
The boy wandered off.
Dave looked again. It was not an eclipse. Not even close.
Back at his desk, Dave checked online to see what people were saying. Others had definitely noticed. Some suggested that it was an unidentified flying object. Only it was not flying but staying in one place. So, an unidentified hovering object? That sounded stupid.

Or a hole. Many people, including some guy on CNN, suggested that it was a hole. Caused by pollution. Others, like that kid outside, said it was only the shadow of the moon: a sort of eclipse only not an eclipse. No one was particularly worried. It would probably be gone in a day or two.

But Dave couldn't take his mind off the spot. There was a window near the water cooler where Dave could see the spot clearly. He made several trips, filling and re-filling his coffee mug with water. Each time he filled his cup, he had to drop a dime into an empty plastic yogurt container with a slit in its lid. After running out of dimes, he dropped a dollar into the container and counted down with each trip. He'd linger, and look out the window at the spot. It hadn't moved but—and this was worrisome—it appeared to have grown larger.

When people walked by, he'd point and ask, Have you seen that? Most people didn't care. A spot? Big deal. Have you seen my inbox? One woman was concerned. Dave didn't know her name or what she did in the office. In fact, he'd never seen her before. But she seemed just as worried as he was. So they shared that.

—My god, she said. What does it mean?
He hadn't thought of it that way. What does it mean? What could it possibly mean?
The woman lowered her voice and said, End of days.
And then she walked off with her head down.

The rest of the day was a write off. Dave had become very adept at pretending to work. He was thankful for computers in the workplace. There was a time when pretending to work required great imagination and effort. Not so anymore. He spread some files out on his desk, opened several windows on his computer and held a pencil in his mouth. When no one was standing behind him, he surfed the web, alternating between searching for answers and playing Tetris. If someone stepped into his periphery, he switched windows and made a face like he was thinking. In this way, his day was no different than any other.

At home, Dave's wife and kids—he had two kids, one of each—were more interested in the black spot that they were concerned. Dave's wife,

Alison, joked that if it got big enough, maybe they could use it as a garbage chute for some of the junk that had been accumulating in the basement.

Instead of laughing, Dave explained how improbable a scenario that was and besides, he pointed out, maybe it wasn't junk to him.

Dave's son Scott found their old telescope in the basement and tried to see if stars were visible through the spot.

—Maybe it's a tear in the space-time continuum, said Scott.

Scott was fifteen and an avid reader of science fiction.

—What's that, asked Sam?

Dave's daughter Sam was eleven, and didn't read science fiction.

Dave waited for Scott to answer but when he didn't, Dave mumbled something about the final frontier and time-travel and the future. Sam said Oh and joined Scott at the telescope.

Before long, Scott had the telescope pointed at the window of a neighbour's house, and he and Sam were taking turns looking into the eyepiece and laughing hysterically.

When Dave asked what they were looking at, they said, The nudists. Dave told them to put the telescope away and get ready for bed.

Later that night, Dave got an aluminum chaise longue out of the tin shed in the backyard. He struggled with it for a few minutes before unfolding it. The hinges were rusty; it hadn't been used in years. There was a time, when the kids were young, that Alison would suntan—or bake, as Dave called it—on the chaise longue while the kids played in a plastic wading pool. Once the kids grew out of the pool, it became the dog's water dish. Both the pool and the dog were gone now. He couldn't really remember getting rid of either. He dragged the chair to the middle of the yard and arranged it to face the black spot. He removed a pack of cigarettes from the pocket of his fleece pullover and lit one with a barbeque lighter. He had officially quit smoking nine months earlier. But unofficially, he had only switched to a lighter brand. That was almost like quitting.

He lay back in the chair and looked up at the sky. It took him a while to find the spot in the dark. But it was still there, visible not in itself, but by the absence of stars in a perfectly round circle of night sky. It looked bigger. He was sure it was bigger. In fact, he was certain that it had almost doubled in size. What he could not ascertain, however, was if the spot was obscuring the stars or worse, somehow swallowing them.

It's not a hole, he thought. It's a mouth. He took a drag from his cigarette and considered this.

—That's crazy, he said. Realizing that he had said this out loud, he looked around at the neighbouring yards. But he was the only one outside.

Three weeks earlier hundreds of birds fell from the sky all over Dave's neighbourhood. Right there in his back yard he'd found nearly three hundred dead starlings. And it was not a very big yard. Before that morning he didn't even know what a starling looked like. Now he could say that he knew what three hundred dead starlings looked like.

Dave woke up early that morning, before the rest of the family, and stood looking out his bedroom window. He rubbed at his eyes and then gently stroked himself. He always woke up with an erection, and he was thankful, considering his age. When the starlings came into focus, he let go of his penis as if it was a dead starling he was holding in his hand. He covered himself with the curtain, and pushed his face up against the glass. He thought it was a prank. Those goddamn teenagers down the street. Coming home from Swiss Chalet with his family the previous night, Dave had stopped to curse at the teenagers for standing in the middle of the road, smoking. The nerve. One of them—a girl!—had called him gramps, and quoted the bible. Well, paraphrased, at any rate. Casting the first stone, and all that.

Dave quickly realized, however, that all of those birds were beyond the scope of a few teenagers, no matter how bored and delinquent.

He dressed and grabbed a few garbage bags from the kitchen. He wanted to remove the birds before the children woke up. It would traumatize them, surely. At first, he gently placed the birds in the bottom of the bag. One at time, as if laying them to rest. But after a dozen, he realized it would take him all day to clear his yard. So after that, he grabbed them two, three, four at a time, and dropped them in the bag, already reaching for the next handful before the first ones hit the bottom. Three and half bags. The birds sat at the curb, cooking in the black plastic bags for two days before they were picked up.

He lit his fifth cigarette off the fourth. He wanted to make the most of this. He could hear Alison inside. Instinctively, he dropped his cigarette onto the grass. She opened a window and called out to him.

—I'm going to bed, she said. Don't stay out there all night. You watching that spot isn't going to make it go away. And don't let that cigarette burn a hole in the lawn. I'd be more concerned about that if I were you.

She shut the window before he could say anything.

He reached down and picked up his cigarette. He looked up. The hole was definitely getting bigger. No doubt about it. He held out his hand and tried to cover the hole from his sight. Its outer edges stretched beyond the width of his hand. He brought his hand down and watched the spot closely. A star on the edge disappeared. And then another. He realized that he was witnessing it expand. It was now the size of a volleyball if held at arm's length. Another star disappeared. And then another. He listened. He was sure he heard a popping sound, like the sound you make when you quickly pull your finger out of the corner of your mouth. A star disappeared. Pop. Another star gone.

And then, like popcorn being popped a block away, the sound grew steadier and the hole grew larger. Poppoppoppoppoppop. Soon the hole was the diameter of a basketball. Within minutes it was the size of his wife's yoga ball. For the first time in he didn't know how long, Dave surprised himself because he felt at peace watching this happen. There was nothing in the world that he could do about it and this—inexplicably—was calming. He lit another cigarette, dropping the lit one from his mouth into the grass without bothering to butt it out. Bigger and bigger. Soon there were no stars left in the sky. Just blackness. The moon never made it past the horizon.

He noticed the edges of the buildings on the horizon thinning out, the buildings themselves growing smaller. The black spot was eating them, too. His neighbours' houses. Their garages. The fences. And soon his own fence was disappearing. He looked at his feet. The toes of his shoes were gone. The laces, also gone. His ankles. His legs. Soon all that was left was his head staring out at nothing. The cigarette was gone. He didn't remember that happening. He looked around and called out.

—Hello?

It wasn't quiet exactly. He heard a soft whoosh-ing sound. Like water or wind, like when you hold a large shell to your ear. It reminded him of that. He imagined a beach, with waves rolling in. He had never been to the ocean, but it wasn't hard to imagine. His wife and kids were there, playing in the surf. He was in the chaise longue, watching them. Smiling. He looked past his family at the forever unfolding ocean. It was sublime.

Soon, Dave couldn't even see the end of his nose. And then he closed his eyes. Or it went dark. He wasn't sure which.

The last thing he heard was a soft pop.

BIRTHS, DEATHS AND MARRIAGES

It was the old story of the sick man falling in love with the hand that smoothed his pillow and chased pain and death away from his bedside. April Morgan, RN, consented to marry Walter Howard, CA, after five months of his near daily pleas for marital union. April's repeated refusals, worn thin by Walter's tenacity and practical reasoning, weakened to the point of resigned but tender consent. She accepted Walter's proposal in the same manner with which she had rebuffed him for all those months: that is, with a sigh and a shrug.

The couple wed in the yard of April's childhood home in a ceremony presided over by the Reverend William R. Fraser. Rev. Fraser was a last minute replacement when the Morgan's family pastor, Pastor John, took ill. Unbeknownst to family and friends, Pastor John had impregnated April out of wedlock just two months previous; and so his illness, whether real or feigned, allowed him the privilege of not overseeing this union, his feelings about which were complicated.

In attendance were April's grandmother Frances, mother Vivian, and younger sister Darla. All three of whom lived in the family home with April. April's father, Mort Morgan, died of pancreatic cancer when April was nine years old. He had been a good man and April had nothing but happy memories of him. His presence was noted in the 'spiritual' sense. Two of April's co-workers, Lorna Booth and Christine Powell, were in attendance. Both women were privately perplexed by the nuptials but publically wished the bride and groom nothing but happiness.

The groom had five guests in attendance, most of whom were acquaintances, really. Two of these guests were gentleman with whom Walter worked at the accounting firm Wilkes, Smith and Wilkes. These two gentlemen were pleased to have been invited. Pleased and, let it be said, rather surprised because neither Edward 'Ed' Franklin nor Cameron 'Cam' Templeton even knew that Walt—as he was known to them—had a sweetheart. And neither man had visited Walt during his long convalescence in the hospital. (Though both had sent Get-well-soon cards at the urging of their wives.) The wives of Ed and Cam, Sue and Lil, respectively, were also in attendance. This would mark Walter's first and only opportunity to make their acquaintance.

Walter also had an uncle in attendance. Uncle Louis was hard of hearing and continually asked the person seated next to him—Walter's colleague Cam—for clarification as to what was being said during the ceremony. At one point, Uncle Louis rested his head on Cam's shoulder and fell fast asleep. Cam allowed him to remain like that for the duration of the ceremony.

Walter's parents, both long deceased, were obviously not present for the nuptials.

In total, there were nine guests in attendance. The remaining guest, Ernie MacGregor, was a neighbour who had not actually been invited to the ceremony but who was allowed to remain because no one was willing to ask him to leave.

Walter's estranged brother Oliver was, to his bemusement, invited to the ceremony but due to a busy and important travel schedule related to his work in international trade, the invitation sat in my– his mailbox until days after the nuptials took place. Oliver has since, however, had the extreme pleasure of making April's acquaintance. And he looks forward to taking on an active role in the upbringing of his brother's child. And perhaps even, who knows, taking on a larger role in April's life. One can dream.

At the urging of April's sister Darla, the couple was registered with Sears, Roebuck and Company. Though April made clear in advance to everyone in attendance that gifts were neither expected nor encouraged.

The reason for Walter's long convalescence is a delicate matter and is, of course, the reason why April was so caring toward Walter and the reason why Walter, upon opening his eyes that first morning following his surgery, fell in love with April in the first place. There was an intimacy involved in her care of Walter, an intimacy he had not been privy to in any other capacity in his life. It was, of course, a professional courtesy, this intimacy, but in his vulnerable state Walter was not cognizant of this nuance.

Walter would die a mere two weeks after his marriage to April. His death was related to the delicate matter that put him in April's care in the first place. April was aware that Walter had no more than six months to live, but due to a misunderstanding at the hospital, Walter was left unaware of his dire prognosis. Walter's doctor had made a note to discuss Walter's situation with him following the surgery but that conversation never took place because the doctor was called away to perform emergency surgery on another patient. The physician who stepped in misread the note and assumed that Walter had been made aware of his prognosis. April, having read the file, was well aware of the situation. And while her actions might be construed as cruel, her intentions were honourable. Somewhat honourable. April wanted to offer Walter a last chance at happiness before his untimely demise. She also wanted to offer her unborn child the opportunity to be born in lawful wedlock. An opportunity Pastor John was unwilling to provide.

    The same guests attended the funeral. The marriage was never consummated. Six and a half months later, April gave birth to a healthy baby boy whom she named Walt. Simply Walt.

DIVORCE

In many ways my parents' divorce was perfectly timed. My wife and I were about to embark on a trial separation (her idea) and my father had just moved into an apartment with his secretary (his idea). I needed a place to live and, since my father had been sleeping in the guest room for the past ten years because of his snoring, my mother now had a vacancy. I had arrived that morning with two suitcases of dirty laundry and a messenger bag that held my laptop and some student essays I needed to grade. My father was picking up the last of his stuff later in the week. The guest room was lined with packed boxes of all sizes. I had to move some aside just to get into the room.

—What does he have in all of these boxes? I asked my mother.

The house hadn't seemed any less cluttered when I arrived.

—This and that, my mother called from the kitchen. Clothes, she said. Books. His ships-in-bottles.

—You must be happy that he's taking those with him.

I looked more closely at the boxes; not one had been labeled fragile or this side up.

—I'm not not happy about it.

I placed my suitcases next to the blanket box at the foot of the bed. A blanket box my father had built in the basement of this very house. I wondered if he had packed up all his wood-working tools. Surely he wouldn't have a workshop in his new apartment. I made my way into the kitchen.

—So men still run off with their secretaries? I asked.

—Office assistant, corrected my mother. And she works in the office next door to your father's.

—Right. They still do that, then?

—You tell me, Jeremy.

—What's that supposed to mean?

—Oh simmer down, she said. I'm only kidding.

My mother looked at me and rolled her eyes.

Anne and I were still sorting through the logistics of our separation. We have two young children, a dog, a car. A house. Neither one of us wanted to be the one to move out. But it was decided that it made more sense for Anne to stay and for me to leave. Anne is a teacher. Primary. Although, she has been on leave for the past year.

She was doing yoga on the living room floor when I left in the morning. The kids were eating toast and watching TV. They barely acknowledged me when I said good-bye.

—Namaste, I said to Anne.

—Go to hell, she whispered.

I looked at the kids to see if they had heard her. They hadn't.

I waited outside for my cab to arrive.

As for my mother and father, no one was exactly surprised when they announced their divorce. As far as I know, my father had never cheated on my mother before. And while their marriage didn't exactly appear to be loving—they had very little in common; they slept in separate rooms and occasionally took separate vacations—they did manage to stay married for over thirty years. I thought they had found a way to make a marriage work, to make it last.

So embroiled was I in my own drama, I barely registered the end of their relationship. But I was worried about my mother, about how she was taking all of this. She appeared abnormally calm.

—Are you in shock? I asked.

She poured coffee into two mismatched pottery mugs. My mother was not old, like some of my friends' mothers. She still looked young, vibrant. Her hair was grey, yes, and she wore age-appropriate clothing but she had a youthfulness to her, to her walk, to the way she carried herself. She kept active; she was especially social. She regularly hosted a book club; she taught piano lessons to children in her house; she took pottery lessons at the local community centre. She rode her bike everywhere. She abhorred the word senior.

—Am I in shock? Your father didn't die, Jeremy. He fell in love with another woman. It happens all the time. Your father and I haven't had sex in over ten years. He had to go somewhere to satisfy those needs. There's only so much masturbating a sixty-one-year-old man can do.

—Jesus, mom.

She gasped and brought her hand to her mouth.

—Oh my God! Old people have libidos!

She shook her head and placed the mugs of coffee on the table.

When I was a teenager, I refused to let my mother talk to me about sex. I'd change the subject, I'd cover my ears and hum, I'd leave the room. There was never any question that my father would be the one to have the talk with me. If it was going to happen, it was up to my mother. And so her counter-strategy to my evasiveness was to talk to every one of my friends who came over. She'd take them aside, have the sex-talk with them, answer any of their questions, and have them promise to pass some of it on to me. Sometimes these friends showed up expressly to speak with my mother. Later, with Anne, my mother would take her aside, talk to her about sex, give her advice. I told Anne to cover her ears and hum, to think of England. But Anne loved my mother. They could sit and talk for hours.

My mother took a sip of her coffee. There was still steam coming off the top.

—You are such a prude, she said. I have no idea where you get that from. Not from me. And certainly not from your father, Mr. Anal. And I don't mean retentive.

—I'm going to pretend I didn't hear that.

She put down her coffee mug and placed her hands on her hips.

—Listen, she said. If you're going to live under my roof like some overgrown man-child who brings his dirty laundry to his mother, then you're going to have to put up with conversations that contain strong language and adult-themed content.

She smiled, clearly pleased with herself.

—Well maybe we can ease into it, I suggested. My... emotions are still pretty raw. I'm an open wound.

—What you are is melodramatic.

—I think I have a right to be.

—Do you?

—I'm going to look around in the basement, I said. Is Dad taking his tools?

My mother rifled through the junk drawer in the kitchen. She came out with a stack of Post-it notes and handed it to me.

—Here, she said. Use these.

I took the Post-it notes and looked at them.

—What are these for?

—So you can label everything you want for after the funeral.

I dropped the pad on the table and took my coffee downstairs.

The basement looked much like it always had. Nothing had been packed up or stored away. My father's tools were still on the peg board on the wall behind his workbench. Each tool was outlined in black marker. Not one was out of place. Other tools were arranged neatly on a shelf next to the workbench. A half-finished birdhouse sat on the table. A gift for one of the neighbours, presumably. It was something he did each spring. Every yard on the block must have two or three of these birdhouses by now. There was a bottle of whiskey on the windowsill above the bench. I unscrewed the cap and added a splash to my coffee. I took a sip and looked around.

When I was a child, I'd sit on a stool under the window and watch my father work. We wouldn't speak. Or not very much, anyway. Sometimes he'd put the radio on low, an old country music station. And he'd whistle or sing the words he knew. I hated the music, but I liked being down there with him. I set up a woodshop in my own basement three years ago, when my first son was born. But I have no aptitude for it. And besides, I'm too busy to fool around with wood and tools and birdhouses. And my children are too young to sit and watch me work.

I went back upstairs.

—What will you do with Dad's workshop?

My mother was sitting at the table reading the newspaper.

—I told him he could come and build a birdhouse whenever the urge strikes him.

She answered without looking up from the paper.

—Why are you being so reasonable about this?

—What do you want me to do? Tear off my clothes and sob like the ancient Greeks?

She pretended to tear at her clothes and sob—like the ancient Greeks, presumably—and finished up with a bow.

—No, but he wronged you.

—Oh, sweetie, she sighed. Let's go sit in the living room and have a chat.

She folded the paper and pushed her chair away from the table. Before getting up, she looked at me for a long time. Her eyes looked sad—but the rest of her face did not.

—Why are you looking at me like that?
—I'm looking into your soul, she said.
—What do you see?
—Darkness!

She got up and I followed her into the living room. As she passed by the piano, she closed the cover over the keys. I had opened it to play a few chords when I arrived. She gave me a look now as she closed it that reminded me that it was meant to stay closed if it wasn't being played. She only had a few rules, and that was one of them.

All of the furniture in the living room had been updated since I had lived in the house. The carpet had been pulled up and replaced with hardwood. The ancient couch and love seat had been replaced with a modern sectional couch and an uncomfortable chair from Ikea. The style of the room time-traveled through three decades to catch up with the present. The only thing that remained was a bookshelf that my father had built and anchored to the wall. It was lined with books, mostly novels. My mother's. And of course piano music. Sheets and sheets of it.

—Are you going to miss him?
—Your father?
—Who else would I be talking about? Yes, Dad.
—No. Yes. Maybe. I'll miss having a man around.
—I'm here.
—You're not a man, you're my son.
—Thanks.
—I'll miss him, yes. We're having dinner in a couple weeks.
—How can you be so forgiving?
—It's not what you think, she said. We were married for thirty-eight years. He wanted something else. And it made me realize that I, too, wanted something else. Marriage is long and hard, Jeremy. And ours was over long before he met this woman. She just provided the catalyst that we were both waiting for.

—Anne is not so forgiving, I said.
—No? If I were her, I might not be so forgiving either.

By the way she said it, it was clear that she already knew everything.
—I know what happened, she said. You had an affair. You got caught. And Anne kicked you out. It's not an original story. Not even all that interesting. It happens everyday. Four out of ten marriages end that way, you know?

—Is that an actual statistic?
She ignored my question.
—Do you love this girl? This… student.
She made the word sound harsh coming out of her mouth.
—No. It was just a thing that happened.
That was mostly true.
—Just a thing that happened, she repeated.
—She left. It's over. She went back home.
—Where's home?
—Montreal.

She threw her head back dramatically.

—Aha. Well that explains a lot.

—What does that even mean?

—A girl from Montreal. You probably had her pegged on the first day of class. Pun only partially intended.

—That's disgusting.

—Say what you want, but a professor doesn't end up in bed with a girl from Montreal by accident.

—I don't even know what that means.

—If you say so.

I knew exactly what she meant. Zoe was very uninhibited, very adventurous. We did things together that I had never even dreamed of doing.

—Why be so forgiving of Dad and not me? What's the difference?

—How long have you been married, Jeremy?

—You were at the wedding. It was in your backyard.

I am not a sentimental person but I remember nearly fainting when Anne stepped outside and crossed the yard to where I stood waiting. I blinked my eyes as if staring at the sun and had to steady myself. She was resplendent in her white strapless dress. She smiled in a way I had never seen her smile before. There was not a doubt in my mind about what we were about to do. We both giggled during our vows and teared up upon saying I do. We meant every word, though we were probably too young to truly understand.

—How long has it been?

—Seven years.

—What I wouldn't forgive is your exceptionally typical timing. And a student? In the twenty-first century? Do professors still do that?

I had forgotten to log out of my work e-mail. That's how Anne found out. In her anger, she forwarded one of the e-mails to the head of my department. She told me she did not want me in the house. She didn't even want me seeing the kids right now. I said I'd get a two bedroom apartment; they could stay with me on weekends. She said not to bother. I wasn't really in a position to argue.

She said, The worst part is that I'm not surprised.

I asked her not to tell any of our friends just yet. She told me to fuck off.

My mother was speaking.

—I understand the university knows about this. Have they fired you yet?

My throat was suddenly very dry.

—No, not yet.

—I love you. I'll take you in like the stray that you are. But this behaviour... it's shameful. You're better than that.
—How is it any different than Dad?
She took a deep breath and exhaled through her nose.
—How do I put this so that I don't offend your Victorian sensibilities? Your father and I had a relationship that allowed for this to happen, that invited the eventuality of this very thing. We love each other, but we were no longer loving each other. Do you understand the distinction? We needed a change. I'm happy, Jeremy. I'm happy for him and I'm happy for me. This is a good thing.
I shook my head from side to side.
—I'm gobsmacked.
—If you were truly gobsmacked, she said, you wouldn't be using a word like gobsmacked.
I leaned back in the chair and looked up at the ceiling. My mind was blank.
—So as you can see, your situation is very different from your father's. He wasn't having an affair with that woman, Jeremy. He came home and told me he wanted to pursue a relationship with her. He essentially asked for my permission.
She took a sip of coffee and smiled.
—He was a good husband. For a long time. He was always there.
—I was a good husband.
It came out sounding more defensive than I intended for it to sound.
—Were you?
I sat forward.
—I think so.
—You should be certain about something like that. Let's call Anne and ask her– Oh, don't look at me like that. I'm kidding. Was she a good wife? Did she put out?
—Don't be so coarse.
—Okay, fine. Did she *satisfy your sexual needs*?
I could hear the italics in each word.
—Sometimes.
—Did she go down on you?
—I'm not answering that.
—Did you go down on her? That's all a woman really wants: cunnilingus and a massage every now and then. You do that, and she'll be happy. Did you make her happy?
I searched around for my coffee. My mother picked it up off the coffee table and sniffed it. She rolled her eyes and handed it to me.

—Like father, like son. I guess I can cancel that paternity test.

Anne and I didn't speak openly about matters of a sexual nature. We used phrases like 'matters of a sexual nature'. And until now, my mother and I didn't talk like this either. But doors had been opened, apparently.

—I don't want to talk about this with you. All of this makes me very uncomfortable.

—I'm saving you from years of therapy.

—Are you sure it's not the other way around?

She smiled.

—You know what I hate, she asked?

I held my breath.

—The word irregardless. I hate it.

—Or humongous, I said, happy to pursue a new line of thought.

—No, I don't mind humongous. Not one bit.

She held her hands about twelve inches apart and laughed.

—Anyways, I said.

—Is that another example, she asked? Because if it is, I hate the addition of the 's' on that word. It makes one sound so stupid.

—What if it hadn't been an example?

—Let's just assume it was, she said, sweeping her hand through the air. How are the boys handling this?

—They don't have a clue.

She thought about this for a minute.

—They're still young, she said. What is your plan? What are you going to do?

—Now?

—Now. Tomorrow. Next week.

She was looking at me intently, her legs crossed, the coffee mug cupped in both of her hands.

—I have work to do. Final papers to grade. I have an article to finish up for a journal.

—That's not what I mean.

—That's how I deal with things. I keep busy.

—Yes, well. Perhaps you need to be less short-sighted, because this approach doesn't appear to be working for you.

She took a sip of coffee and seemed to continue the conversation in her head.

—If you want my... She began to speak but stopped. She finished the last of her coffee and got up from the couch.

—I have a piano student coming over this afternoon, she said. I want you to keep your hands off her.

—Jesus, Mom. I'm not a pedophile.

—Oh, lighten up. I'm kidding.

She gathered both of the coffee mugs and left the room. I soon heard her washing them in the kitchen sink, placing them on the drying rack. I got up to get the essays I needed to grade. As long as I was working, I could forget about nearly everything else. Nearly. Back in the guest room, it felt like my father's boxes had multiplied. The stacks nearly reached the ceiling, blocked most of the light from coming in the window; they surrounded the bed. I pushed aside a few more boxes to clear a space next to the bed and heard a quiet clinking of glass in one of them. I gave it a light tap with my foot. Clink. I was about to kick harder but stopped myself and sat down on the edge of the bed. There was a disciplinary meeting scheduled for the end of the week. It was possible they wouldn't be inviting me back in September. I removed the stack of essays from my bag and brought them to the dining room. I sat down and looked at the title page of the first essay. It was about *The Divine Comedy*; it was titled "Welcome to Hell."

MY DEAD FATHER

Listen closely, he said. And then my dead father lit a cigarette.

So I listened closely, but all I heard was the paper and the tobacco crackle and burn as he inhaled deeply and slowly from his hand-rolled cigarette.

He was transparent, my dead father. I could see right through him like the smoke he exhaled in silent, muddled clouds aimed at the ceiling. There was no light anymore, so I had another drink.

It was a long time before he spoke again.

It's enough with these tattoos, he said. And the women—I know about the women, Alan. Everyone knows about the women.

You were a ghost to me before you were a ghost, I said. And you don't know jack.

You're right about that, he said. You are right about that.

And then he was gone.

THE FLOOD

It all started when this girl drank carbolic acid and dropped dead in front of my apartment. All because of a lovers' quarrel. At least that's what the papers said. Her boyfriend wouldn't marry her. Some people said she was pregnant; some people said they were cousins. A taxi driver threw her into the back of his cab and drove her to the hospital. But she was DOA. And the boyfriend/cousin? He was MIA. I read about it in the paper. It happened outside my apartment, but I read about it in the paper. That's the kind of world we live in now. At first they reported her name as Selena. But then they changed it to Anna. Either way, I didn't know her. But that's what started it: this girl killing herself right outside my door, and the way she did it, too. That was fucked. I don't know what carbolic acid is, but even the name itself sounds lethal, as if saying it out loud could cause your esophagus to close up and choke you to death.

After reading about this, I headed straight to my best girl's place to ask her to marry me. It occurred to me just like that: in the time it takes to snap your fingers. Because life is short and chicks are messed up sometimes. So I thought it best to take care of my affairs, get my ducks all lined up in a row because I wasn't getting any younger. Add any other cliché you want and it would probably be true.

My best girl's name is Lena. Which is pretty damn close to Selena. Maybe that's how I chose her. Because—and I'm not bragging here but—I had a few to choose from. I may not be the best looking guy, but I do all right.

In other words, I had options.

Chris, short for Christina, was out of the question: she's got fat thighs. And also, she has hairy thighs.

Lynn? Two words: hairy forearms.

Corin: well, she has a weird voice. It's high pitched. I mean, she actually squeals sometimes. And it's too bad because otherwise she's great in bed.

And then there's Paula. Paula is sweet. I like Paula a lot. But she has red hair.

So I just automatically headed to Lena's apartment. It's two blocks east, four blocks south. I could walk it with my eyes closed. Not at first though. It's close, but it's like another world over there. Even the streetlights: they hang differently, they light up the sidewalk differently. And that makes me think of a joke my grandfather told me years ago. This guy, he's drunk, right, and he's looking for something under a streetlight. And a cop comes by and asks the guy, What're you doing? And the guy, the drunk guy, he says, I'm looking for my keys. The cop starts looking around, and he's like, Where'd you lose 'em at? And the drunk guy says, Over there. And he points across the street to where it's dark. The cop is confused. He stops looking, and he asks, Then why are you looking here? And the drunk guy is like, 'Cuz this is where the light is!

This is where the light is. See?

Lena always keeps the lights on in her apartment: all of them. It's like Grand Central Fucking Station. I've never been to Grand Central, but you know what I mean even if you haven't been there either. It's bright. Light on in every room. After that blackout a couple years back, I said to her something about conserving energy, but she'll have none of it. Doesn't care about the dark, cares only about the light. So I went looking in the light.

She was home, always is. Picture this: skinny thighs, practically bald forearms, great voice, nice laugh, and brown hair. Chestnut. And I'll say it, sure: nice enough tits. We have good times, Lena and me. And here's another thing, a piece of advice: take a look at the mother. I swear to god it makes sense. If the mother was nice to look at in her day, and even better if she's still okay, then the daughter's going to keep her looks for a long time. If, on the other hand, the mother is a mad-bitch-whore, then scram. Get out of there fast.

Lena's mother was still pretty hot.

There was a lot of noise coming from inside Lena's apartment when I arrived. I had to knock several times before she even heard me. She opened the door a crack, and I knew right away things were a bit funky. She had sawdust in her hair. Sawdust. This was unusual; this was not normal.

—What're you building in there, eh? I said it like a joke, because I never knew her to build a goddamn thing in her life.

—An ark, she said.

—Oh, yeah, I said. An ark? Mind if I come in and take a look?

I played along here, because—fool that I am—I thought it was a joke.

—Oh, fine, she said, like I was bothering her. Come in and take a look all you want.

There was a problem with her tone right off the bat. But I brushed it aside. Last time we spoke, well, we had a little thing. Nothing big, typical thing between two people who are sleeping together, and one of those people is also sleeping together with other people. But we straightened it out. And besides, I was there to ask her to marry me.

She opened the door nice and slow for the big reveal. And sure as hell: there was a half-built ark in the middle of her dining room. An ark! But small, like a dory. This was an ark for maybe two adults, a couple squirrels. She had cleared everything else in the room out of the way. The table was dismantled and leaning up against a wall, the legs piled up on the floor. The chairs were on her balcony. I could see them through the window, stacked on top of one another.

—What... uh, what's the deal?

I was a little flustered.

—It's coming, she said.

She looked pretty pleased with herself. But her expression changed when she saw that I wasn't impressed.

—What's coming? I asked.

—The flood.

I didn't know how to respond to that. I really thought she was fooling with me.

—The flood, eh?

She nodded and walked around to the other side of her ark.

—Look, I came here to ask you something. A pretty big something. And I'm not sure what the deal is with the ark here, but I have this question I want to ask. So can we go into another room where I don't have to look at that thing?

I nodded towards her ark.

—Fine, she said.

We went into the living room.

There was a goddamn table saw set up in her living room. I had never seen this woman use a screwdriver before. And now she had a table saw in her living room! There was a pile of sawdust on the floor and lumber—lumber!—stacked up against the wall.

—Where on earth did you get that?
—What?
—The table saw.
—It's called a mitre saw.
—Fine. Where'd you get the mitre saw?
—Norm.
Norm is the building's super.
—Can we please go into another room? I asked.

We walked down the hall to the bedroom. And right there on her bed was an outboard motor. Big one. On her bed. Now, I wanted to laugh because the thought of an ark with an outboard motor, that's comical to me. But the thought of an outboard motor on the bed of the woman I was going to marry, that was not comical to me. That was fucked.

—Okay, just tell me what is going on here, will you.
—I am building an ark.
—Okay, I get that. But why are you building an ark.
—There's going to be a flood.

She ran her hand along the outboard, back and forth, like she was in love with the thing.

—And what sort of evidence do you have for this coming flood?
—Read about it.
—Where?
—Somewhere.
—And it's a flood so big you need a boat to escape it?
—Yes.
—You live nowhere near water and you don't know the first thing about sailing.

She stopped stroking the motor, and looked at me like I was an idiot.
—You don't sail an ark.
—Right. You don't sail an ark. Okay, then tell me: what the fuck do you do with an ark?
—You load it up with supplies and wait until the flood subsides.
—Lena. Baby. I'm a little worried, here. I–
—You should be worried. There's a flood coming.

Something occurred to me just then.
—That ark is pretty small, I said. Is it just you going on this trip?
She shook her head.
—Am I supposed to fit on that thing with you?

I laughed a little and I thought: go along with it, see where it leads. She got a little weird though, and walked out of the room.

—Isn't that the thing with arks? I asked, following her. Two of every kind?

She picked up a hammer and started banging at some invisible nail on the side of her ark. I took hold of the hammer and put it on the floor just beyond her reach.

—So?

—There's no room for you. You'll have to build your own.

—But there is someone else going with you on this... thing.

I kicked at the side of her ark. It felt surprisingly solid. And if I wasn't so angry, I would have been impressed.

—I have to get back to work, she said. There's still a lot to do.

—Who's going with you?

She reached for the hammer but I kicked it out of the way.

—Who?

She looked up at me and for a second I could see Lena, the old Lena. And I thought, here comes the punch line. It was all some elaborate prank. And I was ready to laugh because it would feel good to be able to laugh about this.

—Norm.

All the air left me at once.

—What did you just say?

My voice did not sound like my voice.

—Norm. Norm and I are going together, she said.

There were a whole lot of things going through my mind at that point. I don't even know where to begin. The wedding was off. That was for sure. I really wanted to scream. And I wanted to smash the shit out of that ark. I took a deep breath. And I tried to suck all the air out of the room and hold it in my lungs until this thing stopped. She reached for the hammer again, and I let her. She spit a nail out of her mouth—a nail I never saw her put there in the first place—and she started in on the hammering.

I turned and walked out the door.

—One last thing, I said, looking over my shoulder. Just how the fuck are you going to get that boat out of your apartment?

She stopped hammering and looked from the boat to me and then back to the boat. I didn't wait for an answer.

On the way past Norm's apartment, I leaned on the buzzer and waited. He opened the door wearing denim overalls and no shirt. He was holding a clipboard and pen. What a royal douche.

—Oh, hey, he said.

I punched him in the face.

—Have a nice day, asshole. I hope you drown.

Outside on the front stoop, I lit a cigarette and stood there a long time. The sky was filled with dark, heavy clouds that rumbled but barely moved. Lightning flashed high above the clouds like secret fireworks. I once saw the northern lights, the aurora borealis. It was this and that, and all the things they say it is. I wanted to put it in a bottle and cap it and save it for a day like this. A day when I'd open the bottle and all this colour would come out and light up the sky and make everything different, or a little bit better. Maybe that's what that girl thought when she opened the bottle of carbolic acid. If I had a bottle of that now, I'd throw it in Norm's face.

I dropped my cigarette butt to the sidewalk and crushed it with the toe of my boot. Time to make a new start. I looked at my watch. It was still early. There was time to catch Paula before she got off work. I would walk her home, and ask her to marry me. She could dye her hair. We could live happily ever after. It was worth a try.

THE SISTERS

Alana and Wynne lived in the home their father built the year they were born. That was more than sixty years ago. Alana had already left and returned. She'd lived in London and, briefly, Paris. Upon returning to Canada, she settled in Montreal. She visited her family once a year, at Christmas. She never married.

Wynne never married either, but nor did she ever leave; she never saw any reason to leave. She was happy at home, happy being her mother's best friend. Wynne and Iris had their programs and their games, their shared secrets and jokes. And because of this, Wynne took her mother's death much harder than Alana or their father, Herbert. So after their mother died, Alana came home to help out. And then, when their father died just two weeks later, Alana decided to stay in the house with Wynne for a little longer. Or rather, Wynne pleaded with Alana to remain. She even, in one of her weaker moments, threatened to hurt herself if Alana abandoned her. Alana had no intention of moving back into the house but she was worried about leaving Wynne alone; she didn't know what Wynne was capable of doing. So a year passed, and then another.

Every morning, the sisters would walk around the lake at the end of their road. Along the route, they'd take note of birds and wildlife, the changing landscape. Alana kept a notebook to record the names of the birds they saw. Wynne would imitate their calls, whistling quietly as she strolled next to her sister.

It was during one of these morning walks that Alana delicately raised the issue of moving back to Montreal. That's where my friends are, she said. My life is there. You could come with me, she added, although reluctantly. In response, Wynne, who became agitated every time this topic came up, shoved Alana into the lake. She had never done such a thing before; it surprised her to find herself doing it now. Alana was equally surprised and therefore unprepared. What neither woman saw was the large rock that was partly submerged next to the shore. Alana tumbled sideways and hit her head on the rock.

She did not stand up afterwards, wring her clothes dry and laugh about it; she did not pull herself to the shore and berate her sister for such an unkind act. She didn't raise her hand for her sister to help her out of the lake and onto dry land. No, she lay there, her face completely submerged in the murky, weedy shallow water. One foot still remained on the shore. That is the image Wynne would never be able to forget. That one foot, Alana's brown shoe, still dry, still resting on the shore.

Wynne rushed home and called the police. She was waiting for them back at the lake, sitting next to the body of her dead sister, when two officers arrived. She did not tell them exactly what happened. Instead, she said Alana was close to the shore and lost her footing on a slippery rock and then hit her head when she fell. She was trying to get a better look at a heron, explained Wynne. A blue heron catching frogs. Wynne described the heron tilting its head back to swallow a frog just as they chanced upon it. It was right there, she said, pointing.

And it was that detail that convinced the detective who questioned her. Though, in truth, he did not suspect foul play. It seemed quite believable: an old woman slipped while bird watching. Hit her head. And died.

Wynne still walks the same route. Though she has been cautioned to steer clear of the slippery shoreline. And so she does.

THE THREE NAPOLEONS

He was having the dream again. Napoleon Bonaparte and a bear were playing chess on the shore of what appeared to be an island. To their right was a long, narrow garden plot with freshly turned soil, a hoe leaning against a small tree; to their left: a gun-metal grey sea and an undisturbed horizon line. The only sounds came from the squawking shore birds fighting over crabs, the small waves breaking on the beach. As if to taunt the exiled emperor, the bear wore a modest crown on his head. But Bonaparte barely acknowledged the crown, so engrossed was he in the game. He did not appear surprised to find himself playing chess with a bear; though his seat was turned away from the table, as if to enable a quick escape should it come to that. The bear's moves were awkwardly handled, what with his huge paws and long claws, but he managed to hold his own against Bonaparte. With each clever move made by the bear, Bonaparte would curse under his breath and shake his head from side to side. The bear, meanwhile, remained mostly impassive. The only time he raised his head to growl at his opponent was when Bonaparte utilized the obscure *en passant* move with his pawn. Bonaparte quickly explained the origins of this move to the bear, using a combination of hand-gestures and French and Corsican words. Satisfied, the bear sighed, and the game continued. Three moves later, the bear executed a successful *en passant* himself. Napoleon was both frustrated and deeply impressed.

    In the dream, the game always ended in the same manner. The bear lost and lazily tipped himself off of his chair until he was standing on all four paws. Bonaparte would nod and watch the bear retreat into the dense foliage skirting the beach. But on this particular morning, just as Napoleon Bonaparte was about to engage the bear's king in a check, a telephone started ringing. Startled by the ringing phone, Napoleon Bonaparte accidentally tipped the chess board to the ground. The bear became unexpectedly enraged. He raised himself to his full height and growled, exposing his stained and sharp teeth. And before Bonaparte could stand and make his escape, the bear lunged across the table, smashing it to pieces, and threw himself upon Bonaparte in a dizzying fury. Within seconds, Bonaparte's body was bloody and lifeless.

The phone continued to ring.

It was only after the fifth ring that the sleeping Napoleon Roy realized the phone was his own, and it was ringing on the stand next to his head. Damp with sweat, Napoleon picked up the receiver and said, What?

It was a potential customer—or client, as Napoleon Roy referred to them. The man on the phone wanted to come by right away; he said he really needed a chainsaw, and fast. The man said his name was Charlie.

—Who gave you my number? Napoleon asked in his croaky morning voice.

—You sold a Remington to my friend Martin—Marty. A red one.

Napoleon turned over in bed and looked at the chainsaws laid out next to him. There were a couple Husqvarnas, a Stihl, a Poulan and he was pretty sure there were at least two small Black & Deckers around somewhere; they may have fallen off in the night. He used to keep the chainsaws on the floor at night and move them up onto the bed in the afternoon—the light was exquisite in the afternoon, when he conducted his business. At some point, he stopped putting them on the floor and just left them on the bed. If pressed, he might admit to liking the weight on the other side of the bed, the smell of oil and gas.

—I don't have any Remingtons right now, he said to the man on the phone.

—I'll take anything.

They arranged a meeting for noon.

Napoleon hung up the phone and reflected on the violent turn of events in his dream. He'd been having the same dream for six weeks and not once had things turned bloody. He tried to dismiss it as an anomaly brought on by the ringing phone, but he was bothered by it. Napoleon was convinced that some secret message was hidden within the dream, some answer to a question he didn't even know he had. So this change in the narrative worried him. Napoleon was also certain that this was not just a dream but some heretofore unknown historical truth: he truly believed it to have actually happened more or less the way it transpired in his dream. He did not know a thing about chess, and yet here he was dreaming about moves like the *en passant* and castling. And Corsican? Forget it, he didn't even know that was a language. And then there was the island: it appeared in his dream just as he found the island of Saint Helena described in a book—a book he read after first having the dream. So convinced was Napoleon Roy, that he spent days in the reference section of the public library scouring history books and biographies and letters to and from Napoleon Bonaparte. So far, his search yielded nothing useful. And despite learning that the island of Saint Helena had no native land mammals, Napoleon refused to stop believing in the possibility of this story. A bear playing chess did sound absurd, he admitted. But if you think about it, it wasn't a huge leap from riding bicycles in the circus to playing chess with Napoleon Bonaparte on an island.

Napoleon was splashing cold water on his face when he heard a knock at the door. He looked at his watch: ten minutes before noon. Charlie was early; Napoleon would take his time getting to the door. After drying his face and hands, he slipped his impossibly tiny .22 calibre mini-revolver into his pocket. This gun of his was the source of no small amount of ridicule from his associates. But he insisted on keeping it and he lovingly maintained the little thing until it positively shone. He checked himself in the mirror and then opened the door to a very tall and very hefty Charlie. They exchanged hellos. Napoleon asked after their mutual acquaintance. The connection was tenuous; Napoleon was a little suspicious. But Charlie was coming from a respected client. So Napoleon led him inside.

    Charlie raised his eyebrows when Napoleon opened the door to the bedroom. But he relaxed when he saw the chainsaws on the bed. The light really was stunning in there at noon.

    —Your name's Napoleon Roy, eh? Charlie gave a cursory glance at the chainsaws.

    —Sure.

Charlie smiled and looked directly into Napoleon's eyes.

—Then you must be the guy with the winning lottery ticket.

Napoleon did not like his tone one bit.

—I don't know what you're talking about.

—I heard from a buddy of mine who heard from his sister who works at the store where that winning ticket was sold, explained Charlie. They say the guy's name is Napoleon Roy. That's you.

    —I never bought a ticket in my life, said Napoleon, almost truthfully.

    But already the gears were turning. He was familiar with the story; everyone in town knew about it. The winning ticket was sold in the town of

H___. And the person or persons who purchased this ticket had yet to claim the winnings. What he didn't know until now was the name on the winning ticket.

—So it's not you, then, Charlie asked?

—Do you think I'd be selling these goddamn chainsaws off my goddamn bed if I was a goddamn millionaire?

—I guess not. She did say he was a bigger guy, said Charlie, sizing up Napoleon.

At five foot six, Napoleon thought of himself as being of average height. It didn't stop him from occasionally wearing thick-soled shoes or standing on his toes in a crowd. He wasn't a bigger guy by any stretch.

—Well, he's a lucky sonuvabitch whoever he is, said Charlie. I heard it's worth a million bucks.

—Listen, said Napoleon, do you want a chainsaw or not?

—I might need to think about it.

—I'm a businessman, said Napoleon. These won't be here tomorrow, even. You want one, you buy it now. That's how I do business.

—Yeah, well, I just don't see one I like.

Napoleon kicked Charlie out and told him to tell Marty to stop giving out his number. It was obvious why he was there. But it did get Napoleon thinking. No doubt about it, a seed was sown in Napoleon's mind that afternoon. But he'd have to act fast.

Back at the library, Napoleon headed straight for the reference department. If you had asked him for directions to the public library two months ago, Napoleon Roy would have popped you one in the nose—just for asking. But now he had no trouble finding his way right to the shelf with the city directories. He pulled out the last published directory and opened it up to the Rs. While he was the only Napoleon Roy listed, there were eight N. Roys. He tore the page out of the book and stuffed it into the pocket of his coat.

On his way toward the door, Napoleon heard someone calling his name.

—Mr. Roy! Stop, please. Mr. Roy!

He looked over his shoulder. It was the reference librarian running to catch up with him. The librarian was a short, bald man who wore spectacles and a suit, always a suit. Napoleon didn't know his name but the man had helped him considerably these past six weeks. Napoleon never explained his sudden interest in the life of Napoleon Bonaparte to the librarian, nor his interest in dream analysis. And the librarian never asked. Napoleon liked this man, though he knew that in any other circumstance, the two would have very little to talk about. He quickened his pace.

—Mr. Roy! Hold up!

Napoleon was almost at the door when he felt a hand on his shoulder.

The librarian was out of breath. He bent over and put his hands on his knees for a moment.

—You're fast, Mr. Roy, but not fast enough!

Napoleon pushed his hands deep into his pockets, trying to muffle the sound of the paper.

—I found something for you, said the librarian.

He held out a very slim and very old book.

—It was misfiled in the overflow shelving in the basement. I was looking for a fencing manual—which I found—when I came upon this small book. It wasn't even catalogued. Must be a donation that slipped through our fingers. I've been able to find out very little about the book or the author but I'll keep searching.

He handed the book to Napoleon Roy. *Napoleon in Exile* by William V. Giles. The cover was worn and cracked, the pages were yellowed and brittle. Napoleon opened it. Published in London, England in 1912.

The librarian was talking.

—To look at on the premises, of course. Not to leave the library! But of course you know that.

—Of course, said Napoleon. Thank you. Thank you very much.

—You're most welcome, said the librarian.

Napoleon stuffed the small book into his pocket and then offered his hand to the librarian.

—Not to leave the library, of course, said the librarian again, indicating the book in Napoleon's pocket with a nervous laugh.

—Of course, of course.

They shook hands.

Napoleon removed the book from his pocket, nearly taking the torn sheet from the city directory with it. He held up the book and smiled.

—I'll just take a seat over there and have a look at it.

As soon as the librarian was out of sight, Napoleon stuffed the book back in his pocket and headed outside. He found a payphone around the corner from the library and pulled out the torn page from the city directory. He dialled the first N. Roy on the list. A woman answered. She said her name was Nathalie Roy. Napoleon hung up before she had a chance to ask why he was calling.

He dialled the second number. And then the third and fourth.

And then the fifth.

—Hunh?

The man on the end of the line sounded out of breath. He heaved out the hunh and inhaled deeply. Napoleon concluded that he must be exceptionally un-athletic. This was promising news.

—Hey, is this Napoleon? Napoleon Roy?

—Uh-huh.

Not wanting to rouse the other's suspicion, Napoleon Roy said:

—It's... the library. Your book is late. And there's a fine. Get it back right away. Or else.

The other Napoleon, already dubbed Lucky by Napoleon Roy, hung up.

Napoleon smiled and circled Lucky Napoleon's name and address on the torn sheet of paper.

Lucky Napoleon lived in the basement apartment of a low-rise on a wide boulevard. The basement apartment had its own entrance at the bottom of a set of stairs to the right of the main entrance. Napoleon Roy crept down those stairs and listened at the door of apartment 1B. He could hear a television inside. And, after several minutes, the unmistakable sound of someone tearing open a bag of potato chips. He walked back up the steps and inched along the wall to the nearest window. Inside, an enormous, shirtless and hirsute man was sitting on a couch, eating chips. The man on the couch was the size of three Napoleon Roys. He had long greasy hair and an unkempt beard. The hair on his chest looked damp and reflected the light of the TV. Napoleon backed away from the window and took a look around. He figured he'd just watch the entrance, and when—and if—the other Napoleon left, he'd make his move. Napoleon had a strong hunch that the lottery ticket was in the apartment. He was pretty sure that Lucky Napoleon was sitting on it until things blew over. He looked like the kind of guy who would do that.

Napoleon Roy crossed the street and sat under a large tree where he could go unnoticed. He thought about his dream. It was really getting to him. Night after night, the same thing. And the fact that he was merely an observer in his own dream really irked him. In a book on dream interpretation, stolen from the library, the entry for bears offered nothing useful. And absolutely nothing about bears playing chess. But how had he, Napoleon Roy, known about those chess moves? The island? The fact that Bonaparte spent time gardening while in exile? All of these things were confirmed in the books he stole and read from the library. He wanted so much to dismiss it as coincidental but it tugged at him and wouldn't leave him alone. In fact, he'd been having trouble concentrating on anything else since first having the dream. He started seeing so-called signs everywhere: a child playing in the street wearing a cheap plastic tiara had Napoleon looking around for a bear.

A man with his hand in the front of his shirt (merely scratching his chest) had Napoleon in a fit, thinking it could be the reincarnation of Napoleon Bonaparte. He could get no relief. None.

Napoleon looked over at Lucky's apartment: still no sign of any movement. He pulled the small hardcover reference book out of his pocket. He flipped through the preface and introduction and started reading at Chapter 1. It took no time at all for the author to mention a few of the more scandalous quotes from the letters to and from Napoleon and his wife, Josephine. Napoleon Roy had come across these letters in several of the other books he'd read, and he always enjoyed them.

Some movement across the street caught his eye. Looking up, Napoleon Roy realized that evening had come on and Lucky was finally leaving his apartment. Napoleon Roy tucked the book back in his pocket and watched as Lucky sluggishly made his way up the steps out of his apartment. At the top of the steps, he stopped and pulled a t-shirt over his head. Taking a deep breath, he continued down the walkway to the sidewalk and then headed east. He moved slowly, and stopped every few steps to clutch his side and take a deep breath. It was painful for Napoleon to watch and more painful for him to wait for this man to leave. Nearly ten minutes later, when Lucky was a block away, Napoleon Roy crossed the street and knocked on the door. No answer. He tried the handle: it was locked.

Back outside, Napoleon squirmed his way through an unlocked bathroom window on the side of the building. The first thing Napoleon noticed was that the bathroom was filthy. The second thing he noticed was that the apartment, though small, was a cluttered mess: dirty clothes and empty food containers covered every surface. The ticket could be anywhere. He went right to work tearing the place apart: he emptied drawers onto the floor, rummaged through closets and cupboards. He even looked in the toilet tank: a waterproof bag would have been ingenious, if not a little risky. In the bedroom, Napoleon went straight for the mattress with a pocketknife, like they do in movies, he thought. Of course, the ticket wasn't there, either.

Napoleon opened the fridge in Lucky Napoleon's tiny kitchen—it was really more of a closet with a fridge and stove. There was a cooked ham on a plate, a carton of milk and very little else. He opened the produce drawers, nothing. He looked in the freezer: nothing. The cupboards and drawers, while unclean, were mostly bare. He dug his hand around inside a tin of instant coffee. No luck. In less than five minutes he had really made a mess of Lucky's already untidy apartment. He closed his eyes and thought for a moment. *He was probably sitting on it.* He walked into the living room and yanked the couch cushions off the couch and threw them on the floor. The ticket was right there, along with all the usual detritus found beneath couch cushions. Napoleon picked up the lottery ticket and brought it to his lips. A millionaire. Him, Napoleon Roy. No more chainsaws, no more shifty clients in the afternoon. Things were about to change for Napoleon Roy. He pulled the reference book out of his pocket and opened it to insert the lottery ticket for safe keeping. Three words made him stop and sit down on the edge of the couch: ursa major fantastica. He didn't know how but he knew what it meant. So it had been true all along. The words were part of a long footnote at the bottom of the page:

> In his long out of print book, *Inside the Mind of Napoleon Bonaparte*, disgraced historian, J. Gibson Milligan, wrote about an incident said to have occurred in the fall of 1820, during Bonaparte's exile on the island of St. Helena. The incident involved the late emperor and a black bear. In his book, Milligan references three letters sent from the island. The letters were never found and it subsequently came to light that Milligan had fabricated at least one of these epistles—even going so far as to produce one such letter, claiming that it was written by Bonaparte's head-servant, Louis Marchand. Milligan soaked the letter in tea and burned the edges—much like a schoolboy might do to reproduce a treasure map. Can absurdity go beyond this? The incident, we shall call it ursa major fantastica, was panned and ridiculed by each and every one of Milligan's peers and contemporaries—including this author. A pathetic example of far-flung imagination in a field of facts. The incident caused Milligan's publisher, Hearth House Press, to recall and 'pulp' nearly the entire print run. A few copies remain in circulation and are collected as an oddity, a punch line to a lame joke. Let it be said that, at one time, Milligan was a historian of great merit. This incident, however, leaves no small blemish on his reputation, reducing him, as we see here, to a mere footnote.

Sitting on the edge of the other Napoleon's couch, Napoleon Roy closed the book and held it in both of his hands. He held it like that for some time, not opening it, not reading it, just holding it. He knew he should get up and out of there as fast as he could. He knew this but remained seated there, thinking. The ticket. The information in this book. The enormous and strange coincidence that was the other Napoleon Roy. He thought that if he just sat there long enough, it would all become clear, somehow. Explained.

—I should go, he said out loud. But he just sat there.

Napoleon Roy didn't move until he heard the click of the door opening. He jumped to his feet, the book and winning ticket held tightly in his hand, and ran to bathroom. He heard Lucky catch his breath and then the slow, heavy footsteps across the floor. Napoleon was trying to climb through the bathroom window—which was nowhere near as easy as climbing in—when Lucky Napoleon stepped into the doorway, sweating profusely, his shirt draped over his shoulder. Lucky stopped and stared at Napoleon Roy, one hand clutching his side, the other holding a glass bottle of pop. Beads of perspiration fell from his face to the floor. A faint squeaking, raspy sound emanated from his throat. Napoleon reached into his coat pocket and brought out his tiny handgun. He pointed it at Lucky with a shaking hand. Lucky didn't react. He might have thought it was a toy; he might not have even noticed the little gun. His eyes were focused on the book in Napoleon's hand. His lottery ticket was sticking out the side.

—Muh, Lucky said, pointing.

Napoleon Roy looked at the book and at the ticket and then back at Lucky.

In that instant, Lucky Napoleon transformed into a wild animal. His mouth opened wider than seemed physically possible and he roared. The man actually roared. The glass bottle fell to the floor and smashed. Pop sprayed across the room in a dizzying mess. Lucky raised his arms and threw himself at Napoleon Roy with all he had. The two men collapsed onto the bathroom floor, with the larger Napoleon on top. With one hand, Lucky was trying to get a hold of the ticket and with the other, he was pushing down on Napoleon Roy's throat. Napoleon was gagging. He tried to move his hand with the gun but it was lodged under Lucky. Lucky was gasping now. His body shuddered, his eyes rolled back. His head fell into Napoleon's face and then all his weight came down on Napoleon at once. That's when Napoleon's handgun went off. He felt a warmth spread across his chest. Napoleon felt Lucky's full weight resting on him, and even though he could feel the pain from the gunshot in his own chest, Napoleon thought that maybe he had shot Lucky instead of the other way around. But it was his blood seeping out, warming his chest.

And then that pain. Unlike any he had ever felt before in his life. Lucky Napoleon was still breathing on top of him; he had had a heart attack. If someone had been looking in the window from outside, it might have looked like Lucky was trying to do a push-up on top of Napoleon Roy. Or that the two men were engaged in a sexual act.

The very strange and surreal nature of all of this was not lost on Napoleon Roy. And he lay there with his head next to the toilet, unable to move—though not because he was paralyzed by the thought of everything that had transpired, not because he was filled with remorse or self-loathing—though he was—and not because he was thinking about that goddamn dream, which was starting to make sense to him now. No, he lay there because he couldn't get up, he could not roll the other Napoleon off of him. And so there he lay, bleeding, dying, in fact, beneath a man with the exact same name as him, a man who had just unintentionally shot him, Napoleon Roy. The ticket, he did think about the ticket. And the book. He could see them, to his left, both covered in blood and sitting in a puddle of pop; the ticket was probably illegible, so too the book.

    Napoleon Roy cried. He cried and he cried and he cried. He cried for the lost ticket and for the book. He cried for having shared his bed with stolen chainsaws for most of the past two years. He cried for having stolen the chainsaws in the first place. He cried for each and every reference book he removed from the library despite the clear instructions to the contrary. He cried for the women he lied to and cheated on. He cried for all the men he had double-crossed. He cried for not attending his father's funeral. He cried for not crying at his mother's funeral. He cried for the sister he had not seen or spoken to in nearly twenty-five years. He cried for the forgotten argument that led to twenty-five years of estrangement from that sister. He cried for all the times he ate a meal in a restaurant and left without paying. He cried for concussing the one waiter who had the balls to chase Napoleon out of the restaurant and down the street. He cried for all the missed and wasted opportunities. He cried for hitting a boy on the head with a baseball bat when he was nine years old. He cried for the son he had never met. He cried for walking out on the mother of that boy when she excitedly announced her pregnancy seventeen years ago. He cried for all the television sets thrown through windows. He cried for the four kittens tied in a bag and thrown into the river. He cried for the one kitten he couldn't bear to put in the bag and instead set free. He cried for that same kitten found dead one day later. He cried for the woman he loved but could not have. He cried for having no one in his life that he could call at a time like this. He cried for each squandered day and night of his life. He cried for not being a better man. He cried for having spent what were surely his last moments crying under the weight of an unconscious stranger.

    Some time later, his eyes swollen and red but finally dry, Napoleon Roy heard sirens. He closed his eyes then, and took his last breath.

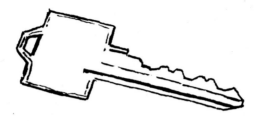

BEATS SITTING IN A CAGE ALL DAY

At exactly six o'clock, the bear locked up his enclosure and hid the key under the welcome mat. Danny, the zookeeper, put the mat there ironically because obviously no one was welcome inside the bear's enclosure. No one except Danny. He was always welcome. Especially if he was carrying a chunk of meat. The bear straightened out the mat and headed for the locker room. He punched out on the enormous old punch clock on the wall and then exchanged his timecard for a slim envelope with BEAR printed on the front. Pay day! He opened up his locker and looked at himself in the small mirror attached to the door. A few grey whiskers. Well, that was bound to happen sooner or later. The stupid crown sat awkwardly on top of his head. Some of the fake diamonds had fallen off. He'd actually swallowed them just for the opportunity to see them sparkling in his turd. Now that would make him feel like a king. He'd been forced to wear the damn crown since the lion died. We need to have a king of the jungle, Danny explained. And you're next in line. Stupid, stupid. But he liked Danny; he knew that he meant well.

    The bear took off the crown and placed it on the top shelf of his locker, next to his helmet. He took his denim overalls off the hook and shook them out. He noted, with some degree of vanity, that they fit a little looser in the hips and belly. All that cycling to work was paying off. He stuffed his pay cheque into one of the pockets and grabbed his helmet. He was unaccustomed to wearing a helmet. But now that his cub was old enough to stand at the window and wave goodbye in the morning, he thought he should provide a good example. He didn't like the helmet; it really made him sweat. And as if it wasn't humiliating enough to be a grown ass bear riding a bike to work, he now had a helmet on his head. But things change when you become a father.

He found Danny in his office and poked his head inside.

—See you tomorrow, Danny.

—Did you get your cheque?

The bear nodded.

—Okay, see you tomorrow, Bear.

The bear got his bike from the garage and headed out. The sun was setting; the heat of the day could still be felt coming off the asphalt. He loved getting home to his family but this ride was sometimes his favourite part of the day. He'd occasionally take the long way, beside the river, and stop for a minute to watch the water and the birds, the kayakers in the rapids. One time he got a can of beer on the way home and cracked it open on a park bench. That was a good day. But when he got home and his wife smelled beer on his breath, she worried that he was developing a drinking problem. Problem? The only problem is I don't do it more often, he joked. But she said it was unbecoming for a bear to sit on a park bench and drink beer. So it only happened that one time.

He rolled up to a red light next to a guy on a bike. To the bear, he looked like the kind of guy who referred to himself not as a guy on a bike but as a cyclist. Tight shorts. Tight shirt. Shaved legs. The bear smiled at the thought of himself dressed up like that and shaving from his ankles to his thighs.

—Great day for a ride, eh? The bear said.

—Yeah, sure, the guy said, not looking at the bear.

A moment passed.

—Beats sitting in a cage all day, said the bear.

The guy nodded and took off as soon as the light changed.

A few blocks later, the bear turned onto his street and rode up to his small bungalow. Sometimes he couldn't believe that this was his life. A house, a family, a job. A job, he had a job. He was the first one in his family to have a job. First one going back, well, going all the way back, as far as he knew. He stood on the curb outside the house. Things change, the bear thought. But he was happy. He was. He reminded himself of this every now and then. This is good, he'd say, this is safe. Beats foraging for berries all day long, am I right? He supposed so. His cub was at the window now, jumping up and down. The bear's heart swelled. Look at that little guy, he thought. What a champ. Everything is new and exciting when you're a cub. His cub had the same ecstatic reaction every single time the bear rode up to the front of the house. That was something.

A second later his wife was there. First her paws and then her snout—she was pretending to fly into view from the side. She smiled and waved with one paw while still pretending to fly. His cub was convulsing with fits of laughter.

This is good, thought the bear. This is exactly right.

Acknowledgements

Thanks to Sarah Caspi, Jon Claytor, Mike Feuerstack, Katie Ward, Lezlie Lowe, Kevin Lewis, Curtis Blondin and David Coyne—for reading and commenting on these stories, and for providing no small amount of love and encouragement. And thanks, too, to my friends and colleagues Nadine McInnis and Moira Farr. I would also like to thank Rita Donovan and John Buschek for all that they do. Grateful acknowledgement is made to the editors of the following magazines, where some of these stories first appeared: *Matrix* (and Pop Montreal), The *New Quarterly*, and *Guérilla*. I am also grateful to SappyFest—where many of these stories were read and also published. And for their support, I would like to acknowledge both the City of Ottawa and the Ontario Arts Council.